WILD THANGZ

A **Winston Chapman** Novel

Copyright © Winston Chapman

BLACK PEARL BOOKS

www.**BlackPearlBooks**.com

D1367453

WILD THANGZ

A Winston Chapman Novel
Is Published By:

BLACK PEARL BOOKS INC.

3653-F FLAKES MILL ROAD – PMB 306
ATLANTA, GA 30034
404-735-3553

All Black Pearl Books titles, imprints and distributed lines are available at special quantity discounts for bulk purchases for sales promotion, premiums, fund raising, educational or institutional use.

Special book excerpts or customized printings can also be created to fit specific needs. For details, write to Black Pearl Books: Attention Senior Publisher, 3653-F Flakes Mill Road, PMB-306, Atlanta, Georgia 30034 or visit website: www.BlackPearlBooks.com

DISTRIBUTION & BULK ORDERING

Contact: **Black Pearl Books, Inc.**
3653-F Flakes Mill Road
PMB 306
Atlanta, Georgia 30034
404-735-3553

Discount Book-Club Orders via website:

www.BlackPearlBooks.com

ISBN: 0-9728005-2-2   LCCN: 2004111871

Publication Date: September 2004

Cover Credits

Design: CANDACEK. (WWW.CCWEBDEV.COM)
Photographer: PATRICK PRIOLEAU (FRONT COVER)

          CHARLES A. BROWN (BACK COVER)

ACKNOWLEDGEMENTS

First and foremost, to my lovely wife for inspiring, cheering and pushing me to the finish line, AGAIN!. You are the world to me! I don't know why you can't see that you're too good for me – but I ain't gonna schedule no eye-doctor appointment for you. I love you baby!

My Publisher, **Black Pearl Books Inc.**, the best publisher in the urban fiction game!!!

To My Author Friends: **Eric Jerome Dickey** - Thanks for your insights and linking my website! **Mark Anthony** (*Author of Dogism*) – You're the next big thing in urban fiction – Believe dat! *Dogism* is the shiznit! **SW Smith** (*Author of The Connection*) – Keep the courage and continue standing up for what's right in the game. Readers: Don't sleep on her skillz! And of course, **Mysterious Luva** (*Author of Sex A Baller*) -- You're blowing up!!!!

Special Shouts To: Charles & Suzette Brown - Without your support, none of this would've been possible! Also, **Maurice Hooks** and da gang at **N.B.E.** for all the laughs and excellent service! And, Ken Johnson, Esq.

Cover Designer: Candace K. -The best book-cover and website designer in the game! (www.ccwebdev.com)

To the **Black Book-Clubs** – Much love goes out to you. Thank you for making *"Caught Up!"* your club's book-of-the-month selection and for inviting me to attend your meetings – I had fun!

To all the **Black Bookstores, Chain Bookstores and Street Vendors** across the country that have loyally supported me -- Thank You!

To various **Media**: Radio, Newspapers, Magazines and Newsletters – Thank you for your reviews, interviews and promotion.

To My Boyz: Gary Beasley, Terrance Hurst & B-Wood (Brandon Woodard)

To The Readers: Thank you for all the e-mails and for making *"Caught Up!"* an Essence Magazine & Black Issues Book Review Magazine Best-Seller!

To My Entire Family: Thanks for the support, patience and understanding of what it really takes to be successful in this game.

WILD

THANGZ

Chapter One

The loud clacking sound caused my shoulders to jerk out of pure nervousness, as I lifted my head and glanced over to three empty seats next to me -- seats that were supposed to have been filled.

I was dressed in the finest conservative business attire that I had in my closet and my hair was flawless.

Ordinarily, I'd be feeling good about the way I looked today and about having so many eyes on me. But, it was definitely not an ordinary day. Today's reason for my special costuming had robbed it of its meaning. It was just plain necessary.

Though I'd been pre-warned that today wouldn't be a long day, it didn't diminish the fact that I hadn't heard someone call me by my full name, Jazmyn Reneé Wallace, since high school home-room roll-call.

The next words out of my mouth would be the most important sentence that I'd ever utter. My shaking voice struggled and cracked as I vocalized a simple two-word response.

Less than two years ago I was basking in the warm sun of Negril, Jamaica with my girlfriends, Trina and Brea, on a College Spring-Break vacation.

We'd been a best-friends-trio since our freshman year at Spellman College in Atlanta. All of us were now sophomores.

"Look at Trina's scandalous ass!", Brea smirked to me at the sight of Trina shamelessly walking up to us from the sandy beach.

Trina had a dynamite body and was never one to cover it up. Today was no exception as she paraded her thick-self up the sand, skirt-wrap in-hand, on her way to the grass-hut bar where Brea and I were seated, still dripping wet from her ocean swim.

Brea and I giggled while witnessing the domino-effect of every guy's head turning as she swayed by them in her fluorescent yellow bikini that contrasted her jet-black skin.

"If this were a highway, you know she'da caused an accident!", I replied back to Brea just before Trina made it to us.

"Ahhhhh! That felt good!", Trina referred to her impulsive ocean dip. "I told you, you guys should've come with me."

"Umm, Trina. You do know that skirt-wraps are meant to go around your waist?", Brea humorously scolded Trina for bringing her bikini-only-covered booty back to us, along with the attention of the entire beach.

"Whatever", Trina countered, as she ordered a drink from the bar after showing identification that she was of legal drinking age, which was 18 in Jamaica.

Trina had always been a strange one. Though she looked every bit the part of the ultimate *sistah-girl*, we swore that there had to be some blonde hair somewhere in the roots of her braids, 'cause at times, she had white-girl tendencies. None more evident than today's impromptu swim. She was the only black person that I knew that would do that. It was like she'd been issued her black skin and didn't know that as a black woman she was suppose to look good by the water, but not actually be in it.

I had always assumed the reason for Trina's country-white-girl behavior was because she was from Savannah, Georgia, a small southern community about 250-miles southeast of Atlanta. Despite being born and raised in Georgia, her speech was absent of the southern twang and as proper as a news anchor's, enunciating every word. Clear evidence of her privileged private school up-bringing.

Brea, on the other hand, was from the hood – Brooklyn to be precise. Though her rougher edges had been smoothed a bit because of her year and a half at college, it wasn't wise to let her model-like beauty fool you. She still had that fire that could come out at any moment, if provoked. Brea was sort of a mix of Alicia Keys and Mary J. Blige.

I guess the best way to describe Brea is Sophisticated-Ghetto. At 5'8, with legs for days, and hair that could be worn curly or straight on a moments notice, Brea's outer-appearance was statuesque and refined. Brea always dressed in the most stylish of garb, no matter what the occasion. At the same time, she wasn't against smoking the occasional blunt or fighting some hoochie in the street outside of a house party. Most people knew of her only one-way, either as Sophisticated or Ghetto. As her friend, I knew both sides very well.

Our trip to Jamaica had been courtesy of Trina's dad, who owned a car dealership in Savannah. As a gift to Trina for her 3rd-consecutive semester with a 4.0 grade point average, she could take two-friends with her to Jamaica.

Her dad was always giving her gifts like that. Sometimes, me and Brea would be a little jealous, 'cause our parents definitely didn't have it like that.

My parents were former musicians that started a cleaning service late in life. Brea's mom had just graduated from nursing school and her father was a night-shift security guard at a New Jersey rail yard.

Part of my envy was rooted in growing-up working in the family business cleaning houses that I wished that we lived in. I'm sure it was a similar situation for Brea. Of course, we weren't quite as jealous when airplane tickets also had our names on them. Or, when we'd catch a ride with Trina in her Navigator, to a UGA (University of Georgia) party in Athens.

The three of us were very different and to outsiders, they might not see the reason for ourfriendship.

Back on Spellman's campus, our group had several

"Yeah, well, what-evah. I don't care, I want me a piece of that!", Brea proclaimed.

"How you just goin' call it? This ain't saving seats on a bus. How do you know that we don't want him?", I playfully started an on-purpose argument with Brea just so that we'd be entertained by her response.

"Bitch please. You can go after him if you want to. We'll just see who gets him", she smiled back at me as she pulled her bikini top outward to show more cleavage.

Spreading the material of her top so far apart that Brea was nearing nipple-territory, if she so much as sneezed.

She wasn't serious at all about competing with us over Donovan. Brea'd be one to say, let's all fuck him. But that's one of the things I liked about her, her sense of humor.

"Y'all know I got the advantage while we're seated", Brea added referring to her better cleavage. "And Trina, don't you even think about standing-up, faking like you're going to the bathroom when he comes back out".

Brea had our stomachs hurting from laughter.

This reminded me of last year's Spring-Break in Miami, which was also courtesy of Trina's dad. Just by being friends with Trina, unknowingly Brea and I were receiving Spring-Break scholarships.

Like last year's trip and for that matter, any party that we went to, Brea was always the first one to hook-up with a man. Sometimes I wondered if it was totally coincidental.

When Donovan returned with our water, Brea turned on the sensuality big time.

"So what do you recommend, Donovan?", Brea asked with a glowing smile while flipping her almost mid-back length hair behind her shoulder.

Her newly displayed cleavage didn't go un-noticed as Donovan stammered on his words and clearly was torn between looking at Brea's face or her chest.

As Donovan struggled to describe the day's special, Brea acted as though the noise in the restaurant made it difficult for her to hear him. Deliberately she turned her head sideways and leaned forward as to bring her ear closer. But it was really to entice him by showing him a better view of her breasts.

Brea was a master of this. It didn't faze me at all. I'd seen her do it many times, as had Trina. However, Trina wasn't as cool at playing it off as me. Her smile leaked out in the form of folded lips and turning her head away as she tried to regain composure.

As I watched her repeatedly lean forward and the material on her top slide, I heard a fire-bell sounding siren go off in my head – beep, beep, beep – nipple alert!

I tried to kick her foot under the table to warn her, but I was a fraction of a second too late. Her little-ass pink-tan nipple had already popped out. But she quickly recovered it in her top. The moment was so fast that the exposure lasted only as long as Janet Jackson's Superbowl mishap.

After that, Donovan's lips were now folded-in like Trina's, and I knew that Brea had him.

After all of the time Donovan spent explaining the special and trying to ignore Brea's bosom, she had the nerve to order just a salad.

I ordered the jerk-chicken and Trina had lobster.

The moment after he'd collected our menus and retreated back into the kitchen, we all giggled.

"Brea, you're wild!", laughed Trina.

"I didn't do it on-purpose! I swear!", Brea said sincerely, as she scanned nearby tables to ascertain who else might've gotten a free show.

Though she remained cool throughout the awkward moment, I could see a little redness coming to Brea's light-skinned face. I think she was truly embarrassed.

"I tried to warn you!", I said referring to my too-late foot-kick. "That's what you get for playing around!"

"N-E-way. Well, that's it. Now I'ma have to fuck him. Nobody gets a free look at me without me getting one back", Brea tried to confidently respond.

"Gurll, you talk so much shit!", I laughed.

Trina and I could always tell when Brea was uncomfortable, nervous or embarrassed because she'd always respond more aggressively, trying to regain control of the situation.

"I don't think he even saw it. Right Jazmyn?", Trina lied about as poorly as she'd played cool.

Trina was good-hearted by nature. Sensing Brea's embarrassment she tried to ease her mind with a simple lie. But I knew Brea was far too sophisticated for that.

"Hell yeah he saw Brea's little-girl nipple", I said, tackling the moment head-on with a pseudo insult. "I'on't know how you got those giant-ass titties with little-girl nipples?", I continued to jab at her until my comments finally forced her to give me the finger and respond with an insult of her own.

"You just mad 'cause your nipples are as big as a damn Nicotrol patch!", Brea fired back.

"Bitch"

"Hoe"

"Hey! Hey! C'mon we're friends!", Trina jumped-in because she thought we were being serious.

Trina always never seemed to get it. But I knew how to change situations or soften moments with Brea. And that way, was not the way Trina had tried with small-town niceties.

We ate our late lunch without further incident. But before leaving, Brea managed to coax information out of Donovan about a swimsuit party that was happening later that evening at Club Menagé that was located just two miles up the road from our hotel.

Donovan wasn't sure whether or not he'd be able to make the party because he had to work at his other job at Rick's Café.

We were all shocked that Donovan worked there because we'd just gone to Rick's Café yesterday and none of us would've forgotten seeing him.

Rick's Café was unique for more than its great food. It was built on a cliff-side and from the terrace of the restaurant you could see the most amazing sunset. The sun appeared to be lowered by a string. Not to mention that you could watch courageous cliff-divers doing acrobatic dives into the water below.

Back at the hotel, we congregated into Brea's room. We all had separate rooms next to each other with adjoining doors. Brea's room was the logical congregating spot because hers was between mine and Trina's.

We took turns trying on different bikinis that we'd

brought and used Brea's room as the pseudo cat-walk to get each others opinion before making our final selections.

For Trina, no matter what she selected she looked booty-ful. We convinced her into wearing a bright blue, green & yellow string two-piece flower-print bikini. Mainly because it was cut lower on the hips. We also added a shear skirt-wrap to her ensemble to tone down her booty-ness.

The consensus for me was that I should wear a halter tankini that tied around the neck. The tankini was short, which allowed me to be subtle-sexy by showing a little skin on my stomach and back, without accentuating my lack of bust. I wasn't super small, a 34-B, but not quite a full-B.

Brea's options were limitless. She looked great in every outfit. The only thing we vetoed was a tube-top outfit because of her large breasts, reminding her of the nipple-incident earlier. With a tube-top, we knew she'd spend half the night pulling the top up, especially while dancing. She decided to mix two bikinis. A high-cut maroon bikini bottom with a maroon and gold string bikini top that we tied so securely that at the end of the night, I thought she would have to cut her way out of it with a knife.

After a brief touching up of our hair, we went down to the lobby and waited for a taxi.

Chapter Two

When we made it to Club Menagé all of us were badly in need of a drink to calm our nerves.

The taxi rides in Jamaica were adventures in themselves.

We thought it was bad when we took the minivan taxi from the Montego Bay Airport through the windy dirt roads on the way to our hotel in Negril. But that didn't even come close to riding in the one tonight.

The two-lane dirt roads were so narrow that when taxis traveling in opposite directions passed it seemed like the distance that separated them was the width of a quarter. Not to mention, how fast the taxi drivers drove and the roads were extremely dark. Making it even worse was that they drove on the left side of the road like in England. I had to close my eyes for most of the short ride and just hope that we'd make it.

The club was poppin' that night. We were feelin' the Hip-Hop American Music that was playing, but it had a Caribbean beat mixed in.

"Hey-aayy", Brea danced through the entrance to the beat of a calypso-version of Notorious B.I.G.'s song, *Big Poppa*, with her hands in the air.

I ain't goin' lie, I'd never heard a version like that before so I was waving my hands in the air too.

"Let's get something to drink", Trina shouted over the loud music.

I tapped Brea on the shoulder to let her know and we began navigating through people towards the bar.

"What y'all want?", I asked Brea and Trina, after finally getting the attention of the bartender.

"I'on't know? Something fruity", Brea responded, still busy jammin' to the B.I.G. song.

Trina was occupied as well checking out the scene of the club.

After getting suggestions from the bartender, I ordered three Jamaican Fizzes. I don't really remember what was in it, but it was slushy, tangerine in color and flavor and potent from the very first sip.

Not two seconds after we'd touched glasses in a toast-like manner and taken the first sip, three fellas damn near knocked each other over as they approached.

"How you doin' luv?", spoke the guy who emerged first from the collision to Brea.

"I'm alright.", Brea returned.

"C'mon", he confidently stated with his mouth and his eyes as he reached for Brea's hand to pull her to the dance floor.

The other two guys paused like they were waiting to see if the first guy failed. When he didn't, they attempted to begin talking to me and Trina. But it was too late, they'd already proven that the race was for Brea, so me and Trina gave 'em no game. We weren't gonna be a consolation prize.

"Can you believe that?", Trina twisted her face at me referring to the weak-ass attempt of the two guys who just left.

"Don't even trip about it.", I brushed it off.

"Jazmyn, I'm just sayin', how are they gonna stand right here next to us and listen to the other guy shootin' game at Brea, not say a word to us at all, until after Brea leaves?", Trina spewed intensely.

"Girl, don't even let 'em get your blood pressure up. They're just weak. Drink your drink and forget about 'em.", I urged.

Right on cue, and proving my point, two different men came up to us. One of the good aspects of tonight's swimsuit theme at the club was that the men were shirt-less.

"How are you fine ladies doing this evening?", spoke one of the mid-20's men to me in a subtle Jamaican accent.

"Fine", we both sung back in unison.

Besides being fine, I liked their style. The way they'd walked confidently over to us without trying to play it off by looking away. They stared directly at us the entire time as they approached.

They were both tall, 6'2 or so. The one closest to me was dark chocolate, hair cut so close you could almost call it bald and had a body that had my nipples hardening. Plus, I

15

loved his voice. It was deep-sounding, but not quite a bass-sound, yet a very full-resonant voice.

"My name is Simeon and this is my boy, Jamal", he said extending his hand to me in a gentlemanly fashion.

I was thrown off as his friend Jamal said his hello because his voice was clearly American.

"I'm Jazmyn and this is my girl, Trina", I returned unable to contain a smile.

Part of the reason for my grin was that as I shook his large hand I couldn't get out of my mind the myth of what large hands meant.

"Jazmyn. A pretty name for a pretty lady.", Simeon complimented.

"Thank you.", I blushed back.

"Jaz, we're going to the dance floor. Watch my drink?", Trina informed me of her plans with Jamal who I assumed had been just as charming to her as Simeon was to me.

"Yeah, I'll watch it.", I guaranteed as I placed a cocktail napkin over the top of Trina's glass.

"Are you from Jamaica?", I couldn't help but ask.

"Why?"

"'Cause you have a Jamaican accent"

"Actually I'm from Houston."

"Houston?", I jumped-in out of disbelief.

"Yes, Houston. My parents grew-up in Jamaica and I still have some family here. But, I was born in Houston, after my family moved to the States."

"I would've sworn you are from Jamaica"

"I get that a lot. I don't really hear the accent myself. I suppose that I got it from my parents."

"So what brings you to Jamaica?", Simeon questioned.

"Me and my girls are on Spring-Break. How 'bout you?", I'd said without thinking about how revealing my age to him would impact me.

Momentarily, he did pause before responding, because I think that he thought I was older.

"A little business, but mostly a vacation. Jamal and I work together and he'd never been to Jamaica, so here we are", he said cooly, but I still could tell that he was pondering something in his head.

Fortunately, he wasn't immediately deterred by my age. It wasn't like I could guarantee that Trina wasn't giving our ages away to Jamal anyway. So there was no sense in lying.

"What university are you attending?", he asked as a prelude to the next question I knew would follow to ascertain my age.

"I'm a sophomore at Spellman College in Atlanta", I responded, saving time by answering both questions, the one he'd asked and the one he was about to ask.

"Oh, Spellman, hmm, that's a good school", he said as though he was thinking about the academic program of the school. But, I knew the *hmm* in his sentence had more to do with the sophomore part.

There was a moment of silence, as I allowed him the opportunity to decide whether or not he was going to continue pursuing me, by turning my attention to the dance floor.

Brea was really startin' to show-off her *skillz* on the dance floor, but the mysterious man that whisked her away was holding his own as well. Even people dancing next to them were admiring their flirtatious moves as Brea turned it around and backed it up on him. And he didn't back away at all, playfully pretending to be spanking her ass with his hand, as Brea smirked appreciation for his confidence with a smile looking over her shoulder back at him.

Trina wasn't a bad dancer either, but not as good as Brea. Her dancing was less risky in style, mostly swaying of the hips with the occasional bounce. It was more suited for a Blue-Lights-In-The-Basement party.

"I'm sorry, Jazmyn, I should've asked you, did you want to dance?", Simeon resumed our conversation.

"Oh, that's okay. No, I gotta watch Trina's drink.", I said relieved that he might still be interested.

"I can buy her another one if you wanted to dance", he generously offered.

Damn, I like this brother!, I thought to myself.

"So, what do you do in Houston?", I innocently asked, but cringed my nose when I thought about the timing of my question.

He'd just offered to pay for a new drink just so that I could dance at my convenience and my question about his occupation I feared could be misconstrued, causing him to think that I was a gold-digger.

"I'm a Marketing Executive for Matthews, Winwood & Associates. We deal mostly with promotional campaigns in the entertainment industry", he spoke with interest.

"Really? It sounds interesting.", I said intrigued, but really I didn't have a clue as to what he was talking about.

18

I think he could sense that I was faking, so he didn't make me suffer and clarified.

"Basically what we do is anything from promotion of music concerts, national television ads for sports, magazine advertising and handle entertainers and athletes career development. We help keep an entertainer or athlete in the lime-light by getting them interviews and endorsement deals", Simeon explained.

"Ohhh, I get it. So, you're like an agent.", I simplified all that he'd just said.

"Yee-ah. Sort-of. But it's not that clear-cut. Many of are clients have agents to negotiate their deals. What I do has more to do with the clients image. It's kinda tough to explain"

Though I still didn't have a full grasp of his occupation, I chose to let it go because it was drawing more attention to our age difference again. It was as though he was my guidance counselor explaining career options.

"So, how long have you been a Marketing...um...Agent?", I said, stumbling to recall his job title.

"Marketing Executive.", he corrected, unoffended by my botching of it. "Four years. I was a Music-major with a minor in Marketing at the University of Houston. After I didn't get drafted, I decided that I didn't want to spend years toiling in the NBDL, National Basketball Developmental League, dreaming about playing in the NBA. So, I chose to begin my career"

"Oh, you're a basketball player?", I said with stars in my eyes.

"Was, a basketball player", he stated.

"That's cool."

Being a former ball-player certainly explained his incredible physique and his confident demeanor when he first approached.

"Was Jamal a ball player, too?", I inquired.

"Yeah, we were college teammates. But now we're going to team-up by opening our own firm next month", he said proudly.

"That's Wassup.", I cheered his entrepreneurial spirit.

"Are you sure, you don't want to dance?", Simeon asked looking at his watch.

It was just a few minutes past mid-night.

"Maybe later. I'm fine just talking", I said with admiration.

"Well, I hate to say it, but Jamal and I have an early-morning meeting with one of our clients, Air Jamaica Airlines, so I'm going to have to get him and we're going to have to leave. But I'd like to get together with you, if you're going to be in Negril for a while?", he charmingly asked.

"That sounds nice. I'd like that.", I said with a slight tilt of my head.

I wrote down my cell phone number and the name of my hotel on a napkin, so that he could call me either way.

Before he left to retrieve Jamal from the dance floor and Trina, he gave me the warmest secure hug, as my hands casually rubbed the skin of his shirtless broad-shouldered back.

His hug wasn't exactly a quick one, yet it didn't exceed the level of our acquaintance. It was perfect, lasted about 6-seconds, his hands gently supported the small of my back and his body felt so good that I didn't wanna let go. To say nothing of the cologne he was wearing that was seductively tickling my nose.

I was in a glowing mood as I watched his sexy ass walk to the edge of the dance floor to get Jamal's attention by pointing at his watch.

Jamal got the message, made his apologies to Trina and guided her by the hand off the dance floor passing right by Brea who was now dancing with a different guy from the one that whisked her away earlier.

Brea was always the life of any party and one never to commit to the first guy that came up to her.

After Jamal gave Trina a good-bye hug that included a peck on her cheek, she was grinning the entire way back to the bar where I was standing.

I was smiling too, 'cause she was walking differently than normal just in case Jamal was still watching her and he was.

When she got to me I answered the question that was on the tip of her tongue.

"Yes, he's watching", I quickly said, with my glass raised to my mouth to shield my lips just in case Jamal and Simeon were long-distance lip readers.

Trina turned around in their direction and we both gave them our most elegant four-fingers-simultaneously-folding-down wave good-bye.

"Gurll, I'm digging them", I confided after I was sure they were gone.

"Me, too. Did you give Simeon your number?"

"Psst. Gurrl now you know….", I said in a manner that indicated she should've known that I had.

"Do you know what they do?", Trina was excited to share.

"Simeon told me!", I returned, matching her enthusiasm.

"Now that's the type of man I'm looking for... A real baller ... You know what I'm saying?", she added raising her hand to receive a gentle high-five.

I gave her dap, 'cause it was true.

At Spellman, we had plenty of guys shooting game at us, but they were always broke. Some of them were college students, so that was understandable, but the movies still cost money.

Brea, Trina and I had stand-by men in our lives. They weren't our real boyfriends. Usually they were older men in their late 20's and had good jobs. They were able to afford things the college boys could not. They provided concert tickets, restaurant meals and clothes shopping money.

I didn't see anything wrong with that. It wasn't like they weren't going after us because they figured that we were easy because we were young college girls. As far as I was concerned they got something and we got something.

"What's poppin'?", Brea said, with an arm around each of our shoulders.

She'd scared the shit out of us because she'd snuck-up on us when our backs were turned.

"Don't do that shit Brea!", I scolded her surprise appearance tactic.

"Quit trippin'", she returned.

"Ain't nothin' poppin' with us. What's poppin' with you, hoe!", I said making reference to the multiple men she'd been flirting and dancing with.

"Now why I gotta be a hoe, bitch? Just 'cause a sistah's getting her groove on? I saw y'all shooting game at those niggas that just left", she informed us.

I hated when she used the word niggas, even though I know she didn't mean anything by it.

"Yes, we were getting better acquainted with some nice brothas", I said extra-formal just to playfully piss her off.

"Get yo' groove on, getting acquainted, same shit! I just came back to tell you the party is about to get krunk. Them niggas are gone now, so it's time to get krunk!", Brea declared.

"What have you been drinking?", Trina asked.

"I ain't had shit but that one drink. I'm just saying, we're in Jamaica...Jamaica!!...We're young and sexy. We need to be doin' our thing, nah-mean?", Brea tried to pump us up.

"Awight, awight. Let's get us another drink", I conceded to her let's-get-wild plan.

Mid-way through our drink the DJ announced the sign-up of the Booty-Shaking Contest that had a $200 cash prize.

"Aw hell naw! Trina, you gotta do it!", Brea slurred encouragement.

"Why me?", Trina questioned.

I just laughed because her response was just reflex.

23

"Why you?? Have you looked at yo' ass lately? Gurll, they giving away 2-bills!! That shit is yours! Can't nobody in here touch you!", Brea spoke the truth.

"You'll win easy!", I chimed in, curious to see if we could convince her to actually do it.

"That's easy for y'all to say.", Trina said with some hesitation.

"What'dya worried about? You don't know any of the niggas up in here. If it were a wet t-shirt contest, I would be all over that shit. I'd get my money!", Brea said with all seriousness.

"You gotta do it. Rep the A-T-L. Rep Spellman. Hell, Rep the whole damn USA, shit!", I said, increasing the urgency.

Brea laughed because I sounded like I was giving a campaign speech about patriotism and not a booty-shaking contest.

Because Trina didn't respond, Brea felt that we'd made enough progress.

"Jaz, go sign Trina up before it's too late. I'll get her another drink", Brea instructed.

Trina didn't tell me not to, so I did.

Chapter Three

It was a little after 1 a.m. when the Booty-Shaking Contest was about to begin.

We'd primed Trina's courage with an additional Jamaican Fizz and she was on the stage with the other nine contestants.

Me and Brea were busy sizing up Trina's competition as the MC had them all turn around to give the crowd of men that gathered at the edge of the stage a preview.

There were a few girls with nice butts, however, only two of them we thought had a realistic chance of actually defeating Trina. The rest either didn't have enough butt or had no business in a bikini let alone a booty-shaking contest.

Before Trina got on the stage we made some last-minute adjustments to her outfit.

The bikini we'd selected for her to wear to the party was cut lower on the hips to tone down her booty which was now a disadvantage in this contest. So, we had her pull the sides up higher to show a little more and remove the shear wrap from around her waist.

Trina was contestant, or as they called it, Booty #7, so she'd be one of the last to dance, which we thought was good for two reasons.

First, it gave Trina a chance to see what the other girls did. And second, going near the end made her more memorable in the judges mind.

Each contestant had 20-seconds to shake their money-maker to one of the medley of derriere-songs the DJ was playing for the contest.

The songs the contestants had to choose from included Mystikal's "Shake Your Ass", "Doin' the Butt" by EU, Sir Mix-A-Lots' "Baby Got Back" and the classic "Rump Shaker" by Wrecks-N-Effect, which is the one we chose.

Just as we suspected, the girls who went before Trina were a little more timid, but with each girl the level of intensity increased as they tried to out-do the one that'd gone before them.

When it was Trina's turn and she walked to the front of the stage and turned her ass to the crowd, a roar went up at the sight of her luscious thang as she waited for the first beat of "Rump Shaker".

"Check baby, check baby, one, two, three, four", began blaring over the speaker and Trina had the fellas raising their hands, hoopin', hollarin' and high-five-ing, as she had her hands on her knees and popped her booty to each and every word of the song. She ended her routine with her knees and hands on the stage, simulating riding that thang.

Brea and I were jumping up and down, 'cause we knew the only way she'd lose was if there was cheating.

While the reluctant remaining three contestants performed their routines that paled by comparison, we were busy looking at the Polaroid pictures we'd paid a club photographer to take of Trina during the contest.

As the DJ announced the 2nd Place Winner, we began celebrating early because the 2nd Place Winner was the girl that had the best shot at beating Trina.

Trina not only won the contest and the $200, but was also given a tiara-crown and a sash that named her Ms. Jamaican Booty of the Year.

We couldn't wait to celebrate with her and eagerly met Trina at the edge of the stage as she was exiting victoriously.

"I told you, gurll!! Can't nobody handle you. I told you!!", Brea proudly proclaimed, giving her a hug.

"You did it, gurll!", I added with my own hug.

Trina attempted to contain a smile, but we knew that she was proud of her accomplishment. And not just because she'd won the contest. Her pride had more to do with conquering her inhibitive-nature. She'd always wanted to be more out-going in public. We knew she had it in her, but tonight she let hesitation fly in the wind and just did it.

A line of brothas was forming around us as we escaped them by walking back to the bar.

Trina removed her sash and set her tiara on the bar as we ordered yet another round of Jamaican Fizzes that were given complimentarily by the bartender as an additional prize.

"I was nervous as hell!", Trina confided.

"Whaaat?? Who in the hell is this? And what have you done with Trina?", Brea playfully asked, referring to Trina's surprising use of a curse word.

"Shut up!", Trina countered by pushing Brea on the shoulder.

"Nobody could tell that you were nervous. You just went up there and did yo' thang! You put it down, gurll!", I said.

"Check these out!", Brea said, handing the Polaroid photos to Trina.

"Oohpp!", Trina said covering her mouth, as she critiqued herself in the photos. "My ass looks fat!"

"Yeah, P-H-A-T, not F-A-T", Brea emphasized.

"Gurll, give me those!", I said, as I snatched the pictures from Trina.

Trina wasn't gonna be satisfied until she turned a good moment into a bad one by putting herself down and I was determined to not let that happen.

"You are Ms. Jamaican Booty of the Year", I said with laughter, "How you goin' act like your butt don't look good?!"

We spent the next 20-minutes shunning away opportunist-guys that kept approaching us only because our girl had won the booty-crown. We knew what was in their minds just by looking into their widened eyes as they advanced.

It was almost 2 a.m. and we'd just decided to leave the club and go back to the hotel, when Brea slyly nudged my side with her elbow and drew my attention to the entrance with a coy nod.

I looked over to see that Jamal was returning to the party and was scanning the crowd with his eyes.

Simeon apparently was not with him, as I surveyed the area around Jamal.

I tapped Trina, so that she'd not be surprised.

"There's your boy", I said, pointing him out from a waist-level point.

Jamal's eyes smiled when they came across Trina and he immediately headed our direction.

"Heyyyy. There you are!", he said to Trina.

"Hi, Jamal", Trina purred back.

"Hi--igh, Jamal", I imitated Trina's singing of his name.

"Hey, Jazmyn", he said, impressing me by remembering my name.

"Mmmph-mmm-mmph", Brea coughed at our failure to introduce her.

"Oh, Jamal, this is my other friend Brea", Trina finished the formalities.

"Nice to meet you, Brea", he said shaking Brea's hand.

"I thought you had a big meeting to get ready for tomorrow?", Trina bated the reason for his return.

"I do, but I never got your number, so I couldn't go to sleep unless I tried to see if you were still here", he charmed her, as me and Brea smiled at his willingness to share his feelings, even in front of us.

Trina hesitated to turn to the bar to get a napkin for her to write her number on because she feared being embarrassed by the crown and sash she thought was still on top of the bar.

Quick-thinking Brea had already taken them off the bar and had them safely hidden in her hand behind her leg.

Trina eye-communicated her appreciation to Brea, without detection by Jamal.

"Thanks.", Jamal said, apparently truly cherishing the digits he'd just gotten by folding the napkin with great care and putting it into his pocket. "As long as I'm here, did you want to dance?", he asked.

"Umm, you know, we were just about to leave.", Trina said looking to us to see if we'd stay awhile.

"Oh. That's too bad. I'd liked to have talked to you some more, seeing as I'm not gonna get much sleep anyway."

Brea and I were Jamaican Fizzed-out and offered no inkling to Trina that we'd stay.

"No, I think I'ma go", Trina said pitifully like she was disappointed that we'd not volunteered to remain.

"Well, I could give you a ride back to your hotel if your friends have to go?", he offered.

Brea was staring hard at Trina and I was curious to hear her response.

Trina looked at us and then began to respond, "Okay, umm, that sounds….."

"Excuse us for a moment, Jarel", Brea jumped in by pulling Trina by the arm.

"It's Jamal", he corrected.

We moved a few paces away from him in a girlfriend huddle.

"Are you crazy? You don't even know that nigga", Brea warned Trina.

"I think he's cool", Trina countered.

"Think? Think?", Brea continued her rampage.

"I agree with Brea, Trina. I think he's probably a nice guy, too. But, maybe you should just hook-up with him tomorrow.", I offered my opinion.

"Y'all so concerned? Why don't y'all stay then?", Trina questioned our commitment.

"Shit! I'm tired. It's two o'clock in the morning. I'm taking my ass back to the hotel!", Brea argued.

"Well, I'm staying. Y'all do what you want, but I'm staying!", Trina confirmed, ending our discussion by turning to walk back towards Jamal.

"This girl's out of her mind!", Brea whined to me in disbelief.

I was prepared to leave because I figured Trina had put her foot down. So what else was there for us to say. She's full-grown. But Brea wasn't quite finished yet.

She walked back to where Trina and Jamal were standing and talking, leaned over the bar to ask for another souvenir cup that the club was giving away and a napkin. She wiped the sides of the cup with the napkin and proceeded to interrupt Trina and Jamal.

"I need you to hold this", Brea demanded of Jamal, handing him the cup.

Jamal did it, but had a confused look on his face.

"Brea, what are you doing?", Trina attempted to protect Jamal.

"Now give it back to me", she ordered to Jamal.

He did. Brea was careful to use the napkin to hold the cup.

"Trina has decided that she's gonna stay, no matter what I say. I just want you to know that now I have your fingerprints on this cup, just in case anything happens to my girl.", Brea said trying to look tough to a man that's 6-inches taller and 100-pounds heavier.

A huge grin came across the face of Jamal at the sight of Brea's tough-acting appearance.

"That's sweet. Don't worry. I'll take good care of your girl", he said, not insulted by Brea's demeanor.

As I watched his poised interaction with Brea, I just realized how handsome he was. I guess I didn't notice before because he'd left so fast earlier to go dance with Trina.

His caramel color skin made his ripped muscles stand out. He had dimples in his face whenever he smiled, hazel eyes and lips like L.L. Cool J.

"I'll see you guys back at the hotel", Trina said, giving us the signal it was time for us to depart.

"Call us when you leave", Brea instructed Trina.

"Take care, Jazmyn", Jamal surprised me with an unexpected hug. "It was nice to meet you too, Brea"

"Umm-hmm", she skeptically returned.

It appeared as though he wanted to be fair and offer Brea a hug, but rightfully so thought better of it and just shook her hand.

Before we departed, Brea leaned over to Trina, "You've got money for a taxi, right?"

"Duh??", Trina said in white-girl fashion showing the $200 cash prize she'd won.

Finally I pulled Brea away from Trina by the elbow and dragged her out the front door, waving good-bye to Trina and Jamal with my other hand.

The taxi ride back to the hotel seemed to last forever, especially because of the Jamaican Fizzes.

Brea and I stood in the hallway using our keys to enter our rooms.

"Call me if Trina calls you first?", Brea instructed.

"I will. You call me if she calls you.", I answered.

"Oh, for sure. No doubt.", Brea promised.

Though we both were exhausted, we knew that we wouldn't completely be able to go to sleep until we knew that Trina had made it back safely.

Immediately, I slipped out of my swimsuit into a comfortable pair of cloth shorts and an old t-shirt, adjusted the air temperature in the room so that I wouldn't be too hot and slid under the covers.

This year's trip was especially important to me because it gave me an opportunity to ponder some choices that I wanted to make in my life.

All three of us were going through some things in our lives.

Trina had been a late-bloomer. It wasn't until her senior year in high school that she'd finished cocooning from a nerdish academia to the diva status she now enjoyed. Though the outside had changed, she still harbored some of the old insecurities.

In addition, her parents were like the black Kennedys of Georgia. Her father, a magna cum laude graduate of Morehouse College, was a well-respected businessman and had many political alliances throughout the state. And her mother, a former Spellman Homecoming Queen, graduated in the top 2% of her class and was now an attorney and lobbyist.

Though Trina was very smart, I knew she felt the pressure of trying to live up to the expectations, not only from her parents, but from everyone on campus who was very familiar with the Whitfield last name.

I think more than completing her Pre-Med degree, Trina yearned to feel ordinary, to be free to make mistakes, to just be herself.

That's one of the reasons I think she enjoyed hangin' with me and Brea. She sure didn't get any special treatment from us. At the same time, we didn't hold her to a higher standard. In fact, we were the ones to encourage her to loosen up and live a little.

For Brea, her situation was a financial one. At the end of this year she'd be losing a scholarship, not because it was her fault, she had 3.2 GPA. It was just due to the lack of donations to the Brooklyn Community Scholarship fund.

Sure, she had other scholarships, but without that one, she didn't know if she'd be able to afford the private school tuition.

As far as she could tell, this was going to be her last year at Spellman.

Brea and I were alike because we would be the first in our families to graduate from college, a pressure that can't be over exaggerated.

It was like our families couldn't wait to have that as bragging material in our respective neighborhoods.

My problem was not one of financial strife like Brea, it was desire. My heart wasn't in it since the very first day I stepped on campus.

I loved music. Loved to sing. And that's what I wanted to do for a living.

My parents were former frustrated musicians that didn't want any of their children to follow in their fruitless footsteps.

They achieved acclaim in the Mid-80's with a duet single that reached #17 on the Billboard charts and a Grammy Nomination. But, due to bad business contracts they never received the money they deserved and were tossed away like used shoes when the style of music changed.

My parents had a sound similar to Peaches and Herb. However, the only evidence of their careers was in photos and music magazine clippings locked safely in a trunk in the attic.

They never talked about it much. Most of the information, I've gotten from my aunts, uncles or their reminiscing friends at informal house parties or barbecue cookouts.

It was clear that they still loved music, though. Just not the music business.

My father was the organist and my mother, the choir director at Good Life Baptist Church. But that was as far as they were willing to go with music. And they certainly didn't want a Wallace child pursuing that dream, especially not their oldest child, me.

I'd been contemplating telling them that I was planning to drop-out of college since the end of my freshman year. But I chickened-out each time.

My parents were working hard and struggled to pay for my tuition, books and room and board so that I could get the full experience of college by living on-campus.

Also, my parents were every bit as anxious as Brea's family to announce to the world that the Wallace family had a college graduate.

It made me feel guilty sometimes for having my own dreams that were different than their dreams for me.

I'd already won several music competitions in the local area and had even been selected to advance in the Atlanta-area local *American Idol* competition. That is, until my dad vetoed my being distracted from college, by trying to continue to Los Angeles.

I would have had to make a commitment to take some time off from school before I even knew if I made it to the finalist level.

I was angry at first because I couldn't understand why he'd step on my opportunity. But after none of the Atlanta-finalist made it to the national level, I wasn't as mad. Yet, I still wondered, would I have been the one?

As I lied in bed, awaiting a call from Trina's safe-return to the hotel, I prepared to totally relax myself from thoughts of informing my parents of my drop-out plans. Thoughts, that were more frequently creeping into my head. An inventive tactic I employed to ease my mind was with one of my newest hobbies, reading.

I turned on the night lamp next to my bed and grabbed my copy of a book called *"Sex A Baller"* by Mysterious Luva that I'd purchased in the airport. The only reason I bought it was 'cause while thumbing through it I saw some interesting Karma-Sutra-like sexy photos in the back of it.

As I stared at the photos in my book and the sexy male model, I kept thinking about Simeon's fine ass.

I was a little jealous of Trina because I wished Simeon had come back to Club Menagé as well.

After needlessly questioning the reason he'd not come back for me as Jamal had for Trina, I was satisfied that it was simply because I had given him my number and Trina had not to Jamal.

Ten minutes of studying the sexual positions in the book that had been given ghetto-fied names and thinking about Simeon had served to make me horny, so I had to put the book down.

I contemplated breaking out my Taiwanese artificial orgasm creator that I had secretly stored in my suitcase. Basically a dildo that was made in Taiwan.

I decided against it.

Instead I turned off the light, slid a pillow between my legs instead and tried to think about something, anything non-sexual.

Chapter Four

It was 3:46 A.M. when I was awakened by the phone ringing in my hotel room.

"Umm, hello", I strained to vocalize.

"Hey Jaz, it's me Trina. I was just calling to let you know I'm in the hotel lobby. I just made it back", Trina whispered, yet sounding wide awake.

"Okay. Thanks for calling.", I said, still groggy.

"Go to sleep. I'll see you in the morning."

"Okay.", I returned, surprised and feeling guilty that I had dosed off for over an hour.

I was about to go back to sleep when I remembered that I'd promised to call Brea when Trina called.

Grudgingly, I leaned over to dial Brea's room number on the phone.

"Mmm..mmm...Hello?", Brea warmed up her voice while answering just as groggy as me.

"Hey Brea, Trina just called from the lobby. She's back at the hotel.", I informed her.

"From the lobby?", Brea woke up more.

"That's what she said", I affirmed.

"Alright, bye", Brea ended our mandatory phone conversation.

I hadn't re-closed my eyes for more than twenty minutes, when my phone rang again.

"Hello", I answered.

"Jaz, it's Brea. Trina brought Jamal back to the hotel with her", Brea whispered into the phone.

"So? How do you know that anyway?"

"I watched them walk by my door through the peep hole", she shamelessly confessed.

"See. That's why I shouldn't tell you shit!", I said sitting up in the bed.

"Come over here! I wanna show you something!", Brea said very giddy.

"Gurll you trippin'! Mind your own business and go to sleep.", I defied.

"No, I'm serious. Come over here now. But make sure you've turned all the lights off in your room first before you come through the adjoining door", she urged.

"Alright. I'ma be over.", I said.

I went to the adjoining door that connected my room and Brea's room. I unlocked my side while I waited for her to do the same on her side.

When she opened her side, I was met with a *shhhh* signal 'cause her index finger was pressed to her lips.

None of the lights were on in her room as she tip-toed in her red silk pajamas top and bottoms to the adjoining door that divided her room and Trina's.

"Trina ain't like you think!", she couldn't wait to divulge, as she wrestled to contain a laugh.

Over her shoulder, I noticed that the adjoining door that led to Trina's room was cracked.

I wanted to be upset that she'd bated me into spying with her, but curiosity got the best of me too.

Now I knew why she was so adamant about me turning the lights off in my room before coming over, concerned that she'd be busted if light seeped from my room into hers and alarmed Trina and Jamal that their door was open.

Brea knelt by the cracked door and I peered in from a standing position over Brea.

Immediately I saw what it was that had Brea so tickled.

Trina was kneeling on a couple of pillows in front of a standing Jamal sucking the shit out of his dick.

I covered my mouth to keep the giggle sound in, releasing it as air through my nose. Brea pinched my leg as a warning that I'd better be able to contain my noise.

I couldn't believe what I was watching.

Trina had always bragged to us that she'd never sucked a dick. Like that was a bad thing or something. And here I was watching her sucking that *thang* like a damn professional street walker. Her head bobbed up and down with speed, even deep-throating it, as she held it in one hand and massaged his balls with the other.

Brea got my attention by tapping my foot and motioning to me with her finger asking me to bend down to her.

"She don't suck dick, huh?", she said rolling her eyes at me. "She didn't just learn that shit tonight! Hell, I don't even suck dick that good!"

I had to move away from the door quickly because her last comment created an urge for laughter so great, I knew my nostrils weren't big enough of an exit for it.

I breathed the laughter out through an open mouth near the bed until I was composed enough to return to the door.

One thing that I was glad to see was that at least Trina made him put a condom on before sucking his dick.

"Oooo, baby", Jamal purred, as he had a handful of Trina's braids in one hand and the other on his own waist.

Trina pulled her mouth off of him to seductively look up at him after he made the noise.

Brea and I both looked at each other with the same thought in our minds.

Once Trina had momentarily pulled off of him and we saw how much dick that extended beyond the grip of her hand, we simultaneously mouthed the word, *Dayyyumm!!!*, to each other.

At first, I figured I'd peek a little at the action and would end-up choosing to close the door. But after seeing that brotha's 12-inches, I was ready to pull-up a damn chair, 'cause I wasn't going nowhere.

Jamal pulled her up to a standing position, then bent down to belly-button level and used his tongue to lick from her belly-button straight up between her breasts, all the way up to her neck that he began nibbling.

My nipples had already begun making impressions in my t-shirt and my breathing became heavy.

Trina swirled her hands around his broad muscular shoulders and head as he bowed low enough to suck on her breasts until her dark chocolate nipples grew.

"Mmmmmm", Trina moaned with her head tilted back, as Jamal took his time on each breast.

Jamal sucked her right breast in his mouth and slowly slid his mouth to the end.

I'd never known it before, but Trina had unique nipples that had extreme extension possibilities. Her peaks grew to about the length and width of a cigarette butt and Jamal was addicted, sucking and flicking them with his tongue until Trina had enough.

As much as my nipples ached from watching, I knew hers had to be sore from the at least 8-minutes worth of attention. My thighs were now inadvertently squeezing together as I was also beginning to get moist.

Jamal turned her back to him, pulled her butt right up against his groin and began caressing up and down her body while Trina's hands rode atop of his.

"Ohhhh...ohhhh...ohhhh", she moaned as his hand first made it down the front of her stomach and between her legs.

I could see from the back-n-forth shaking motion of his hand that he was on clit-territory.

After that deep groaning and thigh-shaking moment from Trina, I was sure Brea would be glancing up at me with a devilish grin, so I looked down only to witness that Brea had unbuttoned her silk pajamas top and was busy massaging her own breast, oblivious to me.

My face instinctively twisted in disdain for her lack of discreetness. Hell, I wanted to rub my damn self too, but I had common sense enough to wait until I was alone in my room.

Brea didn't give a damn. Wasn't ashamed or nothin'.

Though it was difficult to ignore that my friend was masturbating right below me, I returned my attention to the real action at hand. I was determined not to be deterred by Brea into missing this once in a life time opportunity of voyeurism.

Once Jamal had sufficiently warmed Trina up, he guided her into a bent over position with her knees against the front side of the bed and her hands palm down.

Brea and I snickered, as he paused and shook his head in admiration of her ass, before swirling his hands all over it.

Trina adjusted her legs outward preparing for entry.

"Wooo,wooo,wooo", exhaled Trina as she reached behind her with her right hand to his waist to control the initial depth.

Her hand stayed pinned to his hip and her elbow bent like a hinge with each deeper stroke.

Jamal began slowly, then increased depth and pace while adding a swirling pelvic thrust that I'm sure had his dick hittin' all the walls of her pussy.

"Mmmm, mmpph. Oooo, oooo, oooo. Aiygh-yee", Trina begged looking back at him.

He removed her hand from his waist so that he'd have free reign, as he began smackin' dat ass, making it jiggle.

"Give it to me! Give it to me!", he chanted at Trina, with his hands not even holding on to her waist.

His arms were folded across his chest like he was waiting to see what else she had for him.

Trina responded to the challenge by backin' dat ass up faster and harder on him.

"Oooo, OOOOHH! I-iigh!", Trina's sex moans grew with her intensified pace.

"That ain't all you got! C'mon give it to me girl!", Jamal beckoned.

Trina grabbed a handful of the comforter and started backing all the way up on him.

"Ahh, ahhh, ahhhh, AHHH, IYIGH, OOOO, Whoa, Whoa, Whoa, Whoa", Trina's voiced shivered from her body's convulsions.

Jamal had long ago stopped moving to allow Trina to do the work, but now so had she. Well, sort of. Her thighs and ass were shaking and her back was rhythmically twitching up and down.

"You cumming?", Jamal asked.

Trina was still in the middle of her orgasm and couldn't even respond with more than a folded lip, *Mmm-hmmm*.

Jamal allowed her quivering to wane a bit before he flipped her into lying with her back on the bed and her legs straight-up in the air. He held onto her ankles as his *thang* was resting on the top of her pussy.

As Jamal began circling his waist that caused his *thang* to brush back-n-forth across Trina's already sensitive clit, her back arched as she gripped the sheets and her body yet again began trembling.

"Ohhhh, baby, I'm cumming again!", Trina explained with her eyes fluctuating between closed and opened.

Jamal lowered his hips and inserted himself without using his hand to guide.

With each thrust, Trina's head bobbed up and down and her grip on the sheets was as tight a baby's on its security blanket.

Once Jamal had increased to strokes so fast and deep that all of him was disappearing in her, Trina's legs shook more than a dancer's in a Jay-Z video.

"Ahhh, AHhhh, AHHHH, Shee-it, Oh Baby, Uhnnn, Ohhh—Ffff-UCK!", Trina couldn't help but cry out as she was clearly entering her third and most intense orgasm.

This last orgasm was so intense that Trina pushed herself upright with her left hand on the bed and used her right hand to stop Jamal's churning strokes by pressing against his stomach.

Though she'd halted his deep pumps, Trina was still jerking from the after-effects.

"What's up, baby?", Jamal said slightly frustrated because he was just getting it going.

"Wait just a minute", Trina pleaded unconvincingly.

Jamal made sure to remain connected and obliged her request for a time-out.

Once he mentally determined for himself that time-out was over and began resuming, it was apparent that Trina was in no shape to continue.

"Wait, baby, wait.", she again pleaded.

"C'mon baby", Jamal tried to sweet-talk her into resuming.

"I can't handle no more", she finally admitted in uncharacteristic broken grammar.

"Ahh, c'mon baby. I know you're not gonna leave me like this?", Jamal said having been reduced to trying to selfishly guilt her into more sex.

"I'm sorry. I didn't try to do it. I just can't handle any more", Trina said embarrassed, but unrelenting.

She tried to make it up to him by removing his condom and unsuccessfully attempting to hand-stroke him to a *nut*.

We felt bad for Trina and the situation had now become too painful to watch. So, Brea and I slowly closed and locked the door, careful to not have it squeak.

I didn't like that Jamal was making Trina feel bad about the situation, yet I did understand his feeling. Nobody likes being on the verge of an orgasm and everything being stopped. I know I didn't.

I knew Brea felt the same way, though you wouldn't have known it from her comments.

"Can't take the heat you need to get out of the kitchen", Brea flipped out after we'd walked far enough away from the adjoining door.

I knew she didn't mean it that way. That was just how Brea handled uncomfortable situations.

"That ain't even right!", I scolded her lack of compassion. "What if that were you?"

"First of all, that has NEVER been me! I ain't never NOT made a nigga cum! Secondly, IF that had been me I wouldn't've given a damn if a nigga gave me as many orgasms as that nigga did to Trina.", she defied any residue of possible vulnerability in herself.

"That's bull shit! And you know it!", I shook my head to her comments.

"Believe what you want! I would just be like, '*Fuck It!*'", she again tried to convince me.

"You are so full of shit! I oughtta call Jamal over here to watch him wear your ass out!", I unrealistically threatened.

"Call him! I'd have that nigga cummin' so hard he'd leave a trail of it down the hotel hallway", Brea said waving me on with one hand and the other on her hip.

I laughed and it pissed me off that I did. I wanted to still be mad at her for not being sensitive to Trina. But I knew, that's just Brea.

During the voyeurism, my body was in need of some sexual relief and I'd mentally made plans to get that relief using my Taiwanese piece of equipment.

But after witnessing Trina's plight, that urge was replaced by pity for Trina and I would have strange emotions of guilt if I was able to so easily erase those feelings all for the sake of a selfish dildo-induced orgasm.

It apparently wasn't true for Brea, as I could hear her orgasmic moans through the wall, not 30-minutes after I left. She must've been working herself out hard, 'cause I could hear the bed banging the wall.

I flipped around in the bed with my head at the foot of the bed, buried my ears under some pillows and tried to go to sleep.

Chapter Five

During our last two days in Jamaica, Trina never spoke about the incident to us and seemed uncomfortable on the subject of Jamal.

I could respect that and didn't pry, unlike Brea who'd occasionally asked about Jamal to read Trina's face.

She wasn't trying to be cruel, just selfishly trying to bate her into a conversation that might lead to her needlessly hearing details that she'd already witnessed. Usually I stopped her by telling her that it was none of her business.

I was surprised that I hadn't gotten a call from Simeon as he'd promised. Even wondered if Trina's poor performance in bed had somehow affected Simeon's opinion of me.

If it had, I knew that I wouldn't want a guy like that

anyway. Yet and still, I didn't enjoy not knowing whether or not it had.

It was Friday morning when we flew back into the United States landing in Miami, where we'd stay before returning to Atlanta on Sunday.

Our tickets had been booked that way to allow Trina to see her dad while he was in Miami on business for his car dealership.

Mr. Whitfield was an old-school baller. Handsome and very charismatic.

At 6'4, a glowing white pearl smile, just a hint of gray in the side-burns of his mature-fade haircut, and possessing the physique of a man ten-years his junior, Mr. Whitfield didn't look at all old enough to be the father of a college-age child.

Though he was unequivocally a business man, his personality wasn't above using youthful jargon.

"Wassup, y'all?", Mr. Whitfield greeted us at the baggage claim area of the Miami International Airport wearing jeans and a Sean John polo shirt.

He gave Trina a hug first, then gave me and Brea just as equally a daughterly-hug.

"Boy, I tell you – Women sure pack a lot of clothes when they go on trips", he said with a smile waving over a baggage handler to load all our bags onto a cart.

"Daddd-dddy??", Trina said embarrassed by her father's teasing that included me and Brea.

"Well you know we've gotta look good!", Brea teased

back, bordering the line of appropriateness.

"Well, I hope not too good!", Mr. Whitfield backed Brea down with a fatherly glare expression on his face.

I smiled at the fact that he'd shut-up Brea with just one sentence.

"Did you guys have a good time?", he asked as we were now seated in the Jaguar he'd rented as we waited for the baggage handler to figure-out how to get all of our luggage in the trunk.

"Yes, we did Mr. Whitfield. Thank you so much!", I said grateful for his footing of the bill.

"Yes, thank you so much, Mr. Whitfield. I really appreciate it!", Brea attempted to mend her earlier moment with sincere gratitude.

"Good! I'm glad!", he said, as he paid the baggage handler through the window, peeling a twenty dollar bill from a wad of cash as thick as two fingers.

"Buckle up.", Mr. Whitfield directed almost as though we were pre-teens as he prepared to drive away from the curb. "Oh, and before I forget. Here's a little money. I know that y'all are probably broke", he added smiling because he knew that he was right.

He handed each of us three crisp one-hundred dollar bills that he'd already pre-folded at the bottom of the wad.

I felt bad about taking it, because I wasn't his daughter, but he was right, I was broke. Brea did the same and we thanked him genuinely.

"Thank you Mr. Whitfield!", I said.

Brea immediately followed with the identical sentence.

"Girls, listen. You don't have to call me Mr. Whitfield, it makes me feel old", he obliged.

"You are old!", Trina teased her dad.

Trina usually called her dad by his first name, except when she was playing the baby-girl role or wanted something.

"You can call me Mike, Micheal, M-Dawg, whatever!", he said looking back at me and Brea in the rear view mirror and making us laugh. "Anything but Mr. Whitfield".

"Okay, Mr. Whitfield", I accidentally said again out of habit of my parents' training.

Everyone laughed at my blunder. And I did too after overcoming the initial awkwardness of my error.

I had always thought it was strange when I heard Trina calling her dad by his first name on the phone. Just figured that it must be a rich black thing 'cause my parents would have beaten the black off of me if I ever called them by their first names. I don't care how old I got or even if I was selected to read their names as the winners at the Grammys, my announcement would still end with ... *And the winners are my mom and dad.*

We settled into the room that we shared at the fancy art-deco Royal Palm Crowne Plaza Resort Hotel on Collins Avenue.

Mr. Whitfield had a business engagement to attend with a political friend he'd known from college, so we'd arranged to meet for dinner later.

Mr. Whitfield had convinced that college friend to purchase a fleet of vehicles for the Miami Police Department from his Savannah, Georgia dealership instead of using a local one.

I was always impressed because I'd heard so many stories like that from Trina. It was routine to her, but me and Brea thought it was cool that her dad was a baller.

In Jamaica, we'd been able to have our own rooms, but I believed Mr. Whitfield wasn't trying to afford us the opportunity of extreme freedom. At least, not on his watch.

We undoubtedly knew that he could afford separate rooms for each of us. Mind you, none of us were complaining about the luxurious 16th floor two-bedroom suite that we were sharing which included a spacious common living area and a beautiful view of the beach.

Before dinner we intended to make the most of our Miami visit by going to the Bal Harbour Mall in Miami Beach that was also located on Collins Avenue, some 80-blocks up the coast from our hotel.

Briefly we contemplated a beach visit, as it was right outside of our hotel, but decided against it because we'd have all day on Saturday to do that.

We admired the beautiful scenery during the 20-minute taxi-van ride to the mall.

Besides the palm trees that aligned the road, the blue Atlantic Ocean was on the right-side of the van and Biscayne Bay on the left. Along the way, we passed three golf courses that had grass greener than I'd ever seen before. It was so vibrant in color that it almost looked like green carpet.

The Miami mall looked like the United Nations. Every race and nationality seemed well represented.

We window shopped for awhile, usually stopping only at a store that our resident fashion diva Brea wanted to visit.

To witness Brea's lust for clothes one would not have a clue that she was the same person facing financial troubles with school tuition.

It was clear that the three-hundred dollars that Mr. Whitfield had just given us was already burning a hole in Brea's pocket.

I wasn't in the clothes shopping mood because I felt like I must've gained some weight from the four days of great food I'd eaten in Jamaica.

The jean shorts that I had on were usually snug-fitting, but today they seemed to be cutting more into my thighs than normal.

"Brea, you need to get help with your shopping addiction", I advised Brea who was busy sifting through some $800 Prada handbags that she knew damn well she couldn't afford.

"Don't hate the playa...", she raised her eyebrows back at me.

"Whatevah", I said, brushing her off.

After allowing Brea to fantasize for several minutes in the upscale store, Trina became impatient.

"Brea, let's go!", she said.

"Chill. Give me a minute", Brea demanded.

"We're just wasting time here. You know we can't

afford any of this stuff", Trina informed.

"I may not be able to get it today, but I will soon, you just watch!", Brea charged.

"Alright, then let's come back on that day", I said snidely to Brea.

The majority finally ruled and we exited that store and made our way towards the food court area.

Along the way, Brea was stopped at least twice by Latino men who must've thought that she was Latino because they began speaking to her in Spanish.

Brea was from Brooklyn, but didn't know a lick of Spanish. I was more impressed that Brea could seemingly draw guys tryin' to mack from just about any nationality.

While Brea and Trina were busy eating their meals at the food court, I didn't have anything 'cause I was already feeling fat, I received a phone call from a number that I didn't recognize because it had a 281 area code.

"Hello?", I answered.

"Hi. Is this Jazmyn?"

"Yes."

"How are you? It's Simeon."

"Hey, what's up Simeon", I said with more excitement than I intended.

I wasn't mad because he hadn't called me while I was in Jamaica, but I did wonder why not. Also, I didn't wanna send the message that I would be accepting of unfulfilled promises.

Brea and Trina perked their heads up when they heard me use the name Simeon.

I walked away so that I could get a little privacy.

"I'm sorry that I didn't call you earlier, I had an emergency and had to leave Jamaica right after our business meeting.", Simeon apologized.

"I hope everything's alright", I said with concern.

"Yeah, everything is fine. My father has diabetes and we just had a little scare. But he's okay now. He's back at home resting. What are you up to?"

"I'm just hangin' out in a mall. Oh, I'm not in Jamaica anymore", I informed him.

"I know. I called your hotel and they said that you'd checked out. Are you back in Atlanta?"

"No. I'm in Miami now with my girlfriends. I'll be back in Atlanta on Sunday", I responded, pleased that he'd cared enough to call my hotel.

"Jamal and I were planning to be in Atlanta next week to look at some possible office spaces that we may lease for our business."

"Oh, I didn't know that you and Jamal were planning to open your business in Atlanta", I was genuinely surprised.

"Well, it's not final yet. Atlanta is one of the cities we're considering. It's really between Chicago, New York, Los Angeles, Atlanta and Dallas. That's why we're visiting the different cities over the next month. But, Atlanta is the front-runner right now. Office space is reasonably priced and there are many contacts in the industry there. Not to mention, Jamal and I have become use to year-long warm weather. So, we'll see what happens", he explained his plans.

"I think you'll love Atlanta!", I spoke like the chairperson of the Chamber of Commerce.

"You know, I never did get a chance to take you to dinner. I hope you still want to get together?", he flattered me by not assuming that his previous offer in Jamaica still stood.

"Sure, I'd love to get together. Just give me a call to let me know when you're gonna be in town.", I smiled as I responded.

"I will! I promise. I'll talk to you later, Jazmyn. Tell Trina that I said hello.", he finished.

"Alright, I will. Hey, maybe all four of us could go out – you, me, Jamal and Trina?", I suggested.

"Oh...umm...okay...maybe. Why don't we just plan it to be us and play it by ear?", Simeon said sounding flustered by my suggestion.

"Ohh-kay.", I said confused.

"Have a safe trip home.", he rushed to abruptly end the conversation.

"Alright. Bye-bye", I said.

As I closed my flip phone, I paused for a moment to try to put sense to the end of our conversation before walking back to the table where Brea and Trina were already watching me for my reaction. I shrugged off the confusing period of the conversation and reveled in the fact that he'd called me which brought a grin to my face.

"Girl, you are soft!", Brea couldn't wait to comment to me. "You should've cursed that nigga out for not calling you like he said".

"See! You're always talkin' when you don't know what you're talkin' about. Simeon's dad has diabetes and went to the emergency room at the hospital. He hadn't called me because he took an early flight home", I boasted back to Brea.

"Girl, his dad probably ain't even alive", Brea crudely implied that Simeon could be lying.

Trina's face showed how appalled she was that Brea would even say something like that.

I knew that wasn't true. Nobody makes up a lie on their family's health, it's just asking for that to happen.

"Brea, stop", I said with a serious look on my face.

"I'm just saying.....", she attempted to continue.

"Brea, I'm not playing! You take shit too far sometimes!", I warned her.

Brea got the message and let it go.

I really think Brea felt threatened sometimes whenever someone else had a man that showed sincere interest in them. It was almost child-like selfishness, as though everything was cool as long as she was getting the most attention.

It took about twenty minutes of walking around the mall with Trina between me and Brea before the brashness of her comments had subsided in me.

We decide to stop at The GAP store to browse a bit.

"What do y'all think about these?", Brea asked holding up a pair of jeans she'd found that were marked 40%-Off.

"I like them.", Trina commented.

"Jaz?", Brea one-word asked my opinion, trying to squash our lack of communication to each other, yet not apologizing.

I wasn't tryin' to be helpful, still reeling from her earlier statements.

"Fine.", I one-word returned my opinion, having only looked at them for a fraction of a second.

"I'ma try 'em on. Can somebody hold my purse?", she asked.

I walked away.

"I'll hold it for you", Trina volunteered knowing that I wasn't going to.

"Y'all need to make up or something", Trina said to me while Brea was in the dressing room.

That only made it worse because she was talking to me and not Brea like she was scared to tell Brea the same thing. As far as I was concerned it was Brea that she needed to be speaking with and not me.

"Why you tellin' me?", I said with much attitude, attempting to convey that I was someone to fear making arbitrary comments to, just as much as Brea.

"I'm just saying, that both of you are equally as stubborn. Yes -- Brea was wrong for what she said, but...."

"Then you need to be tellin' her that and not me!", I escalated our discussion.

"I'm going to tell her. Whew, you guys are too much!", Trina exhaled frustration.

When Brea walked out wearing the jeans, Trina met her at the mirror as I was several feet away looking at tops.

Though I was trying to ignore them, I could tell that Trina was talking to her about the situation as Brea evaluated the fit of the low-cut jeans in the mirror.

Brea walked over to me and apologized for what she'd said. It wasn't the most heart-felt apology in history. And, it was 30-minutes overdue and prodded by Trina, but at least she did it, so I accepted it.

Brea wasn't sure about the first pair of jeans she tried-on and was considering a different pair that she took to the dressing room to try.

Trina and I rummaged through the sale table for bargains when the cell phone in Brea's purse started ringing.

Trina went to the edge of the dressing room to make Brea aware.

"Brea, your cell phone is ringing", she spoke into the dressing room.

"Just press the ignore button. I'll call them back.", Brea responded.

Trina did as told and rejoined me at the bargain table.

"Who was it?", Brea asked from the dressing room.

"I don't know?", Trina said looking at the display of the phone.

"The name didn't pop up?", Brea asked.

"Uhn-uhn. Just the number. Someone from a 281 area code", Trina said.

I tried to quickly hide the furrowed eye-brow expression that had come on my face after her comments.

Trina had some discounted jeans over her arm, so I volunteered to hold Brea's purse so that she'd not have to wait for Brea to come out before she could go to the dressing room.

Once Trina had disappeared into the dressing room area, I pulled Brea's cell phone out of her purse to look at the phone number of the last call.

It was a 281 number, but not Simeon's. I debated on whether or not I should call it back to see who it was, although I already had a pretty good idea.

Brea emerged from the dressing room unaware that I knew the deal.

"You ain't even right!", I wasted no time saying.

"What???", she said innocently.

"Whose number is this?", I interrogated, showing her the phone.

A guilty look came across her face, as she snatched the phone from me.

"What are you talkin' about? Whose phone number that is, ain't none of yo' business", she attempted to get bold to diffuse the subject.

Her defensiveness served to explain two things at once. First, it put sense to the night I'd thought I heard her masturbating so hard that the headboard in her room was banging against my wall. Now I was pretty certain that it wasn't a solo act. And second, it solved the uncertainty of Simeon at my double-date suggestion during our conversation.

"You fucked Jamal that night?", I directly asked sternly, yet careful not to be loud enough for Trina to hear in the dressing room.

"That's none of your business!", she defended.

"Did you or did you not?!"

"Alright, yeah, I fucked him! So what! He didn't give a shit about Trina anyway!"

I walked in a circle with my hands over my head in disgust.

"I can't believe you! How could you do something like that? And to your friend!", I couldn't stop shaking my head at her.

"I didn't do it to hurt her. I mean, you were there watching it, too. I was just horny and he'd not gotten his orgasm. So ... I just figured ... we'd solve our situations together. I just waited for him to leave Trina's room and opened my door", she offered a weak-ass explanation.

"You didn't mean to hurt her? Well what the fuck do you think would happen if she knew?", I berated.

"Don't act like it's all me. If Jamal cared about her so much, he didn't have to come in my room."

"Can you hear yourself? That's the most stupid thing I've ever heard!"

"Well, what about you Jaz? It ain't like you're so innocent either. You were there watching them having sex", Brea said as though she was subtly trying to deter me from saying anything to Trina.

Her threat was unnecessary, even if I'd not been guilty of the voyeurism. I wasn't planning to say a damn thing. I just hated knowing about it.

"Does Jamal know about that?", I concernedly inquired.

"Are you kidding? Hell, NO! I just acted like I happened to be heading to the hotel vending machine as he was walking by my door", she explained.

I was glad that he didn't know, otherwise Simeon would've known, just as he was apparently already aware that Jamal had slept with a different woman friend of mine.

I knew I shouldn't have let Brea bate me into peeping on Trina and Jamal!, I thought to myself.

If I'd never gone over to Brea's room that night, I'd not feel as guilty as I did right now.

Chapter Six

Late Saturday morning, we ate room service breakfast in the hotel room.

It was a beautiful sunny day, not too warm or too cool. A perfect day for what we'd planned to do, spend some time on the beach.

Despite a restless night over knowing the betrayal that I was harboring from Trina, I'd come to terms that it wasn't going to be a big deal. Trina hadn't talked at all about Jamal, so I figured she wasn't interested anymore. Plus, neither me nor Brea nor Jamal had any reason to divulge the secrets we had in common.

As I walked onto the balcony that overlooked the Atlantic Ocean and surveyed the scene below, amidst the other spring-breakers throwing frisbees, footballs and flying kites, I noticed what appeared to be a camera crew.

I couldn't tell from my viewpoint on the balcony what was going on other than the crew had carved-out a good size space of the beach for themselves.

I figured it wasn't MTV's Spring Break Show because they'd have lots of signage everywhere like they did at last year's spring-break in Miami that we'd gone to.

Brea and Trina were taking a long time to get ready as usual, so I decided to go downstairs to the gift shop to buy some sun-block lotion.

I used to think that sun-block lotion was for white people only until I learned a painful lesson last year that black people can get sunburn too.

That lesson wasn't one that I needed to learn twice. I didn't even know I'd been burnt last year until my skin started feeling tight and dry at the end of the day.

It wasn't until the next morning when I began my normal morning ritual of using *Noxema* cream on my face that I truly understood what white people go through. The *Noxema* burned so badly, it felt like my face had a thousand tiny microscopic razor blade cuts on it and the *Noxema* felt like alcohol.

As I exited the gift shop, I paused because I noticed Mr. Whitfield was across the lobby talking with a woman.

Ooooo!, I thought to myself at first. But then I figured that he was a businessman and she could be a client, wife of a client, who knows.

In either case, I decided I'd leave undetected having had enough of being in the middle of situations like that from just yesterday's turn of events.

Hurriedly, I made my way to the elevators.

"Jazmyn.", Mr. Whitfield called my name even before I had a chance to push the up-button.

"Hi, Mister…. Umm…Michael", I said, remembering to call him by his first name.

I wasn't sure if he knew that I'd seen him with the woman or not.

"You guys are up already? I thought you would've been sleeping in.", he questioned.

It made me feel that he was concerned about whether or not I'd seen him with the woman.

"No, everyone's up. We're going to the beach. I just came down to get some sun-block lotion, that's all", I answered as I pushed the up-button.

"Hey, Jazmyn, do you have a moment?", he asked after watching me push the button.

"Umm…I was just about to see if Trina and Brea were ready", I tried to escape.

"It'll only take a minute", Mr. Whitfield rushed trying beat an elevator becoming available.

"Well..umm…ohh-kay", I hesitated, but didn't know how to evade.

"Good", he said as he motioned for me to follow him to a group of lobby sofas.

We sat down across from each other. I was nervous because I didn't want him to confide anything.

"You know I'ma salesman, right?", he said.

"Yee-ahh", I winced, not knowing exactly where he was going.

"Part of my job as a salesman is to understand and be able to detect human behavior", he commented.

I just nodded having nothing to say.

"I know that I've only known you for a little over a year, but it seems like there's something different about you", he said raising his eyebrows.

"Different about me?", I responded vaguely. "No, there's nothing different about me. Well, I did get my hair colored"

"No, I'm not talking about hair styles or anything like that. You don't seem your normal happy self. How's school going?", he asked.

My lungs exhaled relief that our meeting was of a parental nature.

"School is going good", I smiled back.

"Good! I'm glad of that. It just seems like you have had a lot on your mind the last few times I've seen you. I just wanted to let you know that if there is something that you need to discuss or if I can help you in any way, feel free to come talk to me, okay?"

"Okay."

"Whatever you tell me will stay between us. I won't tell anyone. Not Trina. Not your parents. No one. You have my word on that. I know how difficult it can be talking to a parent and everyone needs someone to confide in", he finished with a reassuring nod of his head and a pat on my knee as he began to stand up.

I'd been so relieved that the subject wasn't of a secret nature that I was about to miss a golden opportunity by letting him walk away.

Mr. Whitfield was like no parent that I'd known. He was cool, yet serious. Fun and real. More like an uncle than a parent.

"Mr. Whitfield, I mean Michael", I spoke, turning around in the sofa I was seated in.

"Yes?", he responded walking back to me and sitting down.

"You know, there is one thing that I've been thinking alot about lately", I entrusted.

"Umm,hmm", he hummed back.

"I've been thinking about dropping out of college"

"Are the classes too difficult?", he asked.

"No it's not that at all. I've got a 3.5 grade point average. It's just not what I want to do", I explained.

"Ohh-kay? Well, what is it that you see yourself doing?"

"Well, I know that you're gonna think that this is stupid, but......", I delayed full disclosure.

"No I won't! You don't have to qualify it, just tell me what it is", he said patiently and with understanding.

"I want to pursue a career in music", I spurted and waited for a negative reaction.

"Okay. You don't know how to tell your parents, that's why you've seemed different."

"Yeah. I guess."

"Well, let me ask you this. Now, don't take my question to mean that I'm siding one way or the other. Could you finish a degree in Music and then pursue your career?"

"Yeah, I guess. But I don't wanna lose the enthusiasm that I have right now by waiting two years to do what I've already been wanting to do since I graduated from high school", I tried to inform clearly.

"Oh, I see. You never wanted to go to college in the first place?"

I could tell Mr. Whitfield was becoming clear on my feelings and emotions.

"Right", I affirmed.

"Dreams are important. And, so are back-up plans. Do you think your parents would not support you, if you decided to drop-out?"

"Yeah…well, no…I don't know? I know that they want me to be the first in my family to have a college degree and they don't want me following in their footsteps making the same mistakes"

"Your parents were musicians?", he asked, nodding his head as though he was putting the puzzle together.

"Yeah."

"Listen, I was the first in my family to graduate from college, so trust me, I know what that pressure feels like. But the difference is, that was my dream as well. This is a tough one. I wish that I could tell you what the right thing to do is, but that's really up to you. You have to live with whatever decision you make. I guess the best advice I could give is to be true to yourself. That way, no matter what happens, you'll have no regrets!"

"Alright. Thanks Michael", I said, still unsure of what I should do.

As I rode up the elevator on my way to get Trina and Brea while trying to put sense to how dedicated I really was to pursuing a music career, I realized that Mr. Whitfield was right about one thing, I did feel much better expressing my dream to someone.

Outside the hotel, we were relaxing on blue cots on the beach, when we were approached by a white man wearing a polo shirt with insignia *Wild Video Productions* embroidered on it.

"Excuse me, I don't mean to bother you young ladies, my name is Tony Vertelli, I'm the Production Assistant for Wild Video Productions. We're shooting a music video today for the band *Blink Twice* and I wondered if the three of you would like to be in it?", he spoke without seeming to take a breath.

"Yeah", Trina immediately blurted out, to the delight of Tony.

I didn't think it was a bad idea, as I looked over my shoulder to the area that was being prepared for the video shoot. Also, I wondered if this was a sign to me about pursuing my music career.

"Hold on a minute. Can you give us a minute to discuss it?", Brea jumped in.

Tony seemed disappointed that Trina's exuberant *yeah* was now turning into a maybe.

"Sure, no problem. Talk it over if you'd like, but I need to know in the next few minutes, okay? Remember, this video will be on MTV and I can promise that I'll get you a lot of screen time", Tony said in a convincing manner.

I'd heard of the band, but just barely. *Blink Twice* was a white suburban type of band, but I didn't really care, it was still a video opportunity.

"If we're going to be in the video I think we oughtta get paid", Brea began our short meeting.

"Brea, they're not going to pay us to be in the video!", Trina expressed. "If we ask for pay, they won't put us in it"

"I'on't know Brea. I see that they already have tons of girls", I said, directing her attention to the bikini-dressed women standing near the shoot scene.

"Y'all don't know shit!", Brea shook her head in disgust.

"Well, I want to be in the video and I don't care about getting paid", Trina conveyed to make Brea aware that she didn't want her to mess that up.

"Have you looked at the girls that they have?", Brea said with raised eyebrows.

Trina and I had, but we turned around again to view them again.

As we turned back around to Brea, she had her hands outstretched.

"Well?", Brea said as though we were suppose to be psychic and know what her point was.

"Well, what?", I asked.

"Y'all wouldn't last one day in Brooklyn. All those girls are white", she informed us of the obvious.

"So what?", Trina hurried, nervous that we might be taking too long with our discussion.

"With all those white girls to choose from, why would he come up to us if he didn't really need us?", Brea explained.

It was something to think about, but it could've meant nothing.

"Who cares? Maybe he just wanted to mix-in black girls into the video, who knows?", Trina inserted.

"Yeah, maybe, but I don't think so. Look how patient Tony is being with us – some girls he just met", Brea responded.

It was true and I was starting to think that Brea might have a point.

"Brea, it doesn't matter", Trina said ready to just tell Tony that we'd do it.

"Hold on a minute, Trina", I said, which brought a smile to Brea's face sensing that I was now on her side.

"What I'm thinking is that we should ask for $500 each to be in the video", Brea suggested.

"You guys are going to mess this up", Trina informed.

"No we're not", I assured Trina. "What's the worst that could happen? They could say no and we could do the video for free if we want to".

I did think that what Brea wanted to ask for was too much, but I hadn't read the reason he'd come up to us in the first place as Brea had, so I conceded to letting her handle the negotiations.

Trina feeling the pressure from both of us, begrudgingly went along with the plan as we walked over to Tony.

"So, what did you decide?", Tony asked.

"Yeah, we decided to be in the video....", Brea began speaking as Tony cut her off.

"Great! I need you to come with me....." Tony began explaining as Brea returned the favor by cutting him off.

"Wait a minute. You didn't let me finish. We'll be in

the video, if we get paid $500 each", she said without a moment of hesitation.

Tony rubbed his chin, as he looked over his shoulder towards another white man standing near the video shoot set who held his hands out in a manner as though he wanted to know what we'd decided.

"Hmmm. Ummm, listen. This is a video that'll be seen all over the world, you guys", he said scratching his head.

Now I clearly saw what Brea had already picked-up on several minutes ago.

Tony must've been told to approach us, by request of someone associated with the band or the director himself.

"Well, if you want us in the video, it's gonna cost $500 each", Brea reiterated to Tony.

I could tell Trina was getting nervous with Brea's Brooklyn-bred hard-ball tactics and was about to make a comment that would surely weaken our negotiation.

I quickly pinched the back of her arm to stop her before she even started.

"Okay, fine. $500 each, but you can't tell any of the other girls what I'm doing for you", Tony agreed with that one condition.

"Fine", we all smiled including Trina who was impressed by Brea's skills.

We went into the office trailer that was on the beach and signed the release forms.

It was very clear that the director wanted the curves and shapes of black women in the video, despite the fact that the band was more of a pop band and that was why he took advantage of the opportunity when he saw us on the beach.

The white girls that had already been waiting for their chance to be in the video hated the prime attention that we got as we were shooting the video. Most likely 'cause they'd seen that we were last minute additions.

I felt goofy at times trying to dance to music that I would never buy, but hey, I was getting paid 500-bucks.

The director placed us closest to the band members, so we'd gotten the most attention from the cameras.

Once shooting of the video had wrapped, Trina and Brea got their cash, ignored the beach, and went back inside the hotel to change clothes to prepare to go shopping with the unexpected loot.

I hung around the set watching the scenes we'd just shot on the monitors and talking with Tony and the director, Martin Creed.

It was an opportunity to learn more about the industry that I was interested in pursuing and no shopping-spree was gonna make me miss a chance to learn or to get a contact in the biz.

As I sat in the trailer with Martin, who was a mid-30's white guy that had a hip-flare to his aura, I explained to him that I was interested in a singing career.

I wasn't sure how much he could help me with my goals, considering the type of band that he was directing the video for today was not in my genre of music.

"I shoot all types of videos, not just pop music. In fact, I shot the *For Real, For Real* video for Nia Moore", he explained, rocking back in his chair with his sun-glasses dangling around his neck.

I was impressed because Nia Moore was one of the

hottest R&B singers in the game today and she had her roots in Atlanta as well.

Martin seemed unimpressed in the revelation that I was a singer and I'm sure that was because he heard that all the time from people with no talent.

Seizing the opportunity, I stood up and began singing Alicia Keys' "*Fallin*" so that he could see that I did have talent beyond the roundness of my booty.

I smiled as I watched him lean forward with interest as I hit every one of the toughest notes in the song.

"Wow!", he said while clapping his hands together. "Do you have a demo?"

"Ummm. No I don't", I replied disappointed that I was unprepared.

"Oh, you gotta get a demo. Here's my card. I'm not a talent agent, so I don't really deal with signing singers to contracts, I just direct videos. But, I could pass the demo around. You've got an excellent voice from what I can tell. Jazmyn, you've gotta get a demo", Martin re-emphasized.

"Thanks", I said while staring at his expensive raised-lettered and gold-foiled business card.

"Hey, you know what? I just thought about something. One of the label guys from *Blink Twice's* record company is suppose to meet me at my room later tonight around 8:00 PM. I can't promise anything and their company might not be the right match for the type of music that you want to do, but it might be a good thing to sing that song for him as well. I mean, who knows? Just a thought", Martin suggested.

Martin and the Wild Video Productions staff were also staying at the Royal Palm Crowne Plaza Resort Hotel.

He wrote down his room number and I agreed to stop by.

I was super excited as I went back to the empty hotel room. Brea and Trina were no doubt already at one of the local malls spending the video shoot cash.

This was just like so many other music success stories that I'd read about in VIBE, XXL and The Source Magazines. I couldn't believe that I could be hours away from a possible record deal.

I ordered some hot lemon tea to help prepare my voice for the make-shift audition and ironed a shape-flattering outfit that I planned to wear.

I was scared to tell Brea and Trina 'cause I didn't wanna jinx it, but I couldn't hold it, so I called them on the cell phone.

Brea was uncharacteristically enthused about an opportunity that didn't include her. And of course Trina was her normal easily excitable self.

I hated that I couldn't call my parents because I knew that they didn't want me anywhere near the music industry. I knew that they would have forbidden me to go to the audition, thereby killing my spirit. So I didn't inform them.

In my mind, I figured that once it was clear to my parents that I had a secure chance for a lucrative record deal that maybe they'd change their minds. I knew that they meant well, but I think they were just being over-protective.

Attempting to get some rest before the audition proved itself to be difficult. I was just that excited about my chance to achieve my dream.

Even darkening the room by closing the shades didn't help.

Though I was restless, I still feared over-sleeping, so I set the alarm clock and left a 6:30 PM wake-up call at the front desk, just in case Brea and Trina didn't make it back by that time.

Brea and Trina made it back to the room a little before 7:30 PM, bearing gifts for me.

I was already dressed and had been practicing for about a half-hour.

I didn't want to wear-out my voice by over-practicing, but I wanted to make sure my voice was properly warmed-up.

The gift Brea and Trina had for me was an outfit for the audition.

"You look good in what you've got on, but maybe try this out and then decide", Brea encouraged.

"I appreciate it so much, but I don't know if I have time?", I said extremely cautious of being on time.

"What time is the audition?", Trina asked.

"8 o'clock. Well it's more like an introduction and audition", I said, trying to relax myself.

"Oh, you've got plenty of time!", Brea urged.

It was true. How long was it gonna take to go to another room in the same hotel? I just didn't wanna put myself in a position to have to rush.

Finally, I conceded and tried on their outfit.

Chapter Seven

Dressed fashionably sexy in Brea and Trina's newly bought outfit, I was nervous as I knocked on Martin's door.

Martin's eyes widened as he appeared to be surprised that I could look equally sexy with more clothes on than the swimsuit he'd seen me in earlier in the day.

With Brea having been on the case, I knew that I looked good in the red top that draped low between my breasts. The bottom of my top was short enough to make my navel visible and show-off my stomach. And the black stretchy-jeans highlighted my curves.

"Hello, Jazmyn", Martin said with a smile as he invited me in.

"Jazmyn, I'd like you to meet Joseph Myers", Martin

introduced me to the man that I assumed was from the record company.

Joseph stood up out of courtesy and shook my hand as we exchanged greetings.

"And, you remember Kelli from the shoot", Martin continued making reference to the white girl that was seated by the table.

I did remember seeing the very busty white-girl at the video shoot, but I never actually knew her name.

She half-hearted smiled a hello and I gave her the same lifeless smile back.

"Have a seat. Make yourself comfortable. We're just having a drink, would you like one?", asked Joseph, offering me a glass of some 1989 Louis Roederer Cristal champagne.

"No. I'm cool", I responded, wondering when I would get the chance to sing.

Other than in music videos, it was my first time actually seeing a bottle of the very expensive $1,000-per-bottle vintage bubbly.

Joseph was handsome for a white man in his early-40's. He had a look that seemed to have been recently converted from a preppy-style. While the clothes he wore may've been of a casual nature, I could tell by the quality of the material that they weren't bought off-the-rack.

Joseph was obviously very intelligent judging by his mannerisms, speech and the way Martin seemed to have the utmost respect.

I was feeling a little uncomfortable as I sat quietly on the bed watching videos on the television as Joseph and Martin talked about all sorts of industry stuff. Kelli wasn't saying anything either as she sat very close to Martin.

Their conversations were filled with laughs and intriguing stories. Often I'd hear them nonchalantly throwing around statements regarding music deals with dollar figures of 6 and 7-digits.

When Joseph went to the bathroom, I waved Martin over to me.

"What's up?", he said sitting next to me on the bed.

"When am I gonna sing for Joseph?", I questioned.

"Relax. I'll bring the subject up soon. You can't seem too anxious, alright?", he assured me.

I stared hard over Martin's shoulder at the nosey big-tittied Kelli who was trying to eaves-drop on our conversation.

I wondered why she was even in the room. She didn't appear to have any talent. If she did, it sure wasn't dancing, judging by her performance at the video shoot.

The longer I waited to sing, the more nervous I got thinking about the importance of the moment. Despite the risk a drink might have on my voice, I decided to have a glass of champagne.

Once Joseph returned to the table and Martin had transitioned the conversation to that of new talent, I got my chance to sing the Alicia Keys song.

The drink I'd had calmed my nerves and I sung it the best I ever had. The jealous look Kelli had on her face fueled my confidence that much more as I belted out notes I didn't even know that I could do.

"Wow! Wow! Incredible!", Joseph applauded my performance.

"I told you!", Martin said, proudly taking credit for discovering me.

Kelli applauded as well, but only to not give away what a bitch she really was.

I didn't know what to say. I just stood there catching my breath.

"Do you have a demo?", questioned Joseph.

"No", I again was sad to admit.

"Are you in a group? Do you have an agent?", Joseph asked his flood of questions that made me feel that he was really interested.

"No, not yet"

"Well, I think that you're dynamite! Simply incredible!", he complimented.

"Thank you", I said with a tilt of my head, then looking over to Kelli who'd smirked negative faces during my performance to try to make me mess up.

My look at Kelli was as to say, *Top that bitch!*

Joseph invited me to talk with him out on the balcony as we sipped another glass of the bubbly.

Mesmerized by the night ocean air and by his repeated compliments, I was feeling very good.

"Jazmyn, listen. I could really help you if you get a demo done for me", Joseph promised.

"I can work on one soon as I get back to Atlanta", I said confidently, though I had no clue where I'd get one done or even if I'd be able to get one done.

"I normally don't do this, but I'm thinking about offering you a developmental deal right now. I'm just that impressed with your talent. Normally, we review demos of an artist and actually see them perform live and even then it's a group decision at the company. But, I might be willing to risk taking some heat to sign you now", Joseph enticed.

I was speechless.

"Well, what do you think? Are you serious about singing?", he continued.

"YES! I'm very serious!", I enthusiastically returned.

"I'll be perfectly honest with you, a lot of singers say that they're serious until they find out how much work is involved. Also, a developmental deal isn't a guarantee that the label will release a CD of your music, but it's the first step in that direction. It's the starting point for every artist. If you show us that you're willing to do whatever's necessary, with your talent, I know that you'll top the Billboard charts. So, what do you say?"

"I'm interested!", I urged.

"Great! Let me just make a quick call to one of the Label Executives and then we'll go discuss this some more", Joseph said pulling out his phone.

I couldn't wait to get back to my room to give the news to Brea and Trina. I wanted to pull-out my cell phone and call them right then, but I didn't wanna look that green.

Instead, I leaned on the balcony railing as I listened to Joseph giving glowing revues of a talent he'd just heard, me.

There seemed to be some hesitancy on the other end of the phone as Joseph had to assure the person on the other phone that he was making a good decision despite my lack of a demo and a group approval meeting.

"I'm telling you, we'll be sorry if we don't sign her now! She already has had other labels talking to her from performances she's done", Joseph spoke confidently while delivering a wink to me.

He spoke a few more minutes and ended his conversation with a huge smile.

"Okay, they've given me the green-light to make this decision. Don't let me down Jazmyn, I had to promise to take responsibility if this doesn't work out", he raised his eyebrows at me.

Things had moved faster than I expected. The moment was surreal.

Joseph led me off the balcony back into the hotel room.

"Martin, Jazmyn and I will be right back. I'm going to get the paperwork to sign her to a developmental deal", Joseph informed Martin.

I didn't know that I was going with him until his statement.

Martin smiled out of pride for the part he'd played and gave me a thumbs-up gesture.

Inside of Joseph's hotel suite, I sat in a chair by the table as he opened his briefcase on the desk and pulled out a developmental deal contract for me to review.

The developmental deal contract came with a signing bonus of $2,000.

"Do I have to sign this now?", I asked.

"Well, yeah", Joseph said seemingly confused as to the reason for my delay.

I didn't want to offend him, but I thought that I should have someone look it over first.

"I don't mean any offense, but shouldn't I have someone look the contract over for me?", I questioned.

"No offense taken. Listen Jazmyn, this is a standard developmental deal contract. It's not the real contract that we'll have you sign once we're going to release a CD on you. So, no you don't really need an attorney for something this basic", he explained.

"I guess what I'm saying is, would it be alright if I have someone look at it before I sign it?", I tentatively requested.

"Do you remember when I asked you if you were serious about singing?"

"Yes."

"Well, I'm not trying to pressure you, but I have a lot of singers that I could sign. I don't have time to waste when what we're talking about is just the developmental deal contract. Not to mention that I just got special permission from one of the Label Executives to sign you without a demo and a group meeting, all because you told me that you were serious. Now I'm not so sure of my decision", Joseph said slightly miffed at my delay as he took the contract back from me and placed it back in his briefcase.

"I've just never done this before, I'll sign it", I conceded.

"I'm not so sure anymore. I mean, if we're going to have this amount of distrust on the developmental deal, what's gonna happen when we're talking about hundreds of thousands or millions?", he inquired.

"I just made a mistake. I'm sorry. I'll sign it", I again attempted to convey.

"How do I know that you mean that this time? How do I know that you're not just saying that because you just realized that developmental deals don't grow on trees? I don't know, let me think about this for a minute before I call the Label Exec back to tell him that the deal is off even though that's going to make me look like a fool", Joseph said plopping down on the edge of the bed, turning the television on with the remote.

I didn't know what else I could say, so I just sat there and waited.

After about 10-minutes of Joseph's flipping through channels without saying as much as a word to me, his cell phone rang. He looked at it and pressed the ignore button.

"That was the Exec, no doubt wanting to know what happened", he whined at me.

Joseph breathed a big sigh and seemed to have subdued his anguish.

"Ohh-kay, Jazmyn, come here", he beckoned me by patting the edge of the bed for me to come sit next to him.

I did.

"If you truly want to make it in this business, the first thing you've got to learn is that you can't let people down. That's just the way the game is played. Everybody has to scratch someone else's back", he educated.

"I'm sorry. I didn't know that you'd get mad", I fought back water in my eyes.

"I'm not mad. Just frustrated a bit", he said wrapping an arm around me at the sight of my welling eyes.

His embrace unlocked the tough veneer I'd tried to project and a tear fell that I wiped with my hand.

"Don't worry. We're gonna sign the deal. You just can't leave me hanging like that anymore, especially when I step-out on a limb for you, okay?"

"Okay", I sniffled back.

Joseph gently glided the back of his finger down the side of my face. My eyes fell to the floor from discomfort.

"You're gonna be just fine. You just gotta trust me", he whispered, as he continued his gliding finger around to my chin and lifted my face in his direction.

Though he'd turned my head towards him, I hadn't raised my eyes.

He leaned over and surprised me with a kiss on my lips. I didn't return the kiss, but I didn't move either. I was just frozen.

His fingers traced the rim of my draping low-cut top that I was wearing.

I knew where this was going, but I was indecisive as to what I should do.

I thought about what Brea might do in this situation, but she was unpredictable. On the one hand, she'd be likely to mess-up a good opportunity by rejecting Joseph's advances. At the same time, she'd always said that she'd not be against fucking someone to get ahead. Her rationale was that if you'll fuck someone for free why is it wrong to do it for something.

Then I thought about my conversation with Mr. Whitfield about going after dreams.

Maybe this is just a part of what I have to go through to reach them, I thought.

During my hesitation, Joseph used his tracing finger

to pull my top outward to allow him to peer down my blouse at my bra-less breasts.

I hadn't given any indication that this was cool with me, but it didn't seem to matter to him.

His right-hand gripped my left breast firmly through my top as he ran his fingers across it until my nipple was firm.

Joseph kissed my neck, as he slid his hand underneath my blouse and began pinching my nipples so hard my face winced.

I'd mentally made peace that I'd already let it go too far to retreat.

As Joseph attempted to remove my blouse, my aiding him by raising my arms was the first sign to him that I was okay with this.

He laid my back to the bed and straddled my middle as he groped my breasts, sucking the nipples with precision, both in technique and in fairness to each breasts. The hard squeezing of his hands combined with his steady sucking of the peak had my nipples the hardest they'd ever been.

I didn't know if it was due solely to his superior experienced technique or had more to do with the fact that he was the first white man who'd ever had his lips on my titties.

"Mmmmph", I couldn't help release, as he flicked my peaks with his tongue.

Joseph pinched both peaks between his thumbs and fore-fingers, pulled straight-up stretching them out and proceeded to shake my breasts while holding onto the nipples.

"Ooooohhh-woooph", I moaned, as I felt a butterfly feeling creep into my stomach and moistness beginning to accumulate between my legs.

His technique was damn good and quickly made me forget that his advance was originally unwanted.

Joseph continued his mouth-love on my breasts as he reached behind him with his right-hand to begin stroking between my legs.

I closed my eyes, folded my lips in as I prepared to endure his grinding hand.

"Mmmm-mmmmph", I groaned with each hand stroke as my eyelids fluttered.

Next, Joseph took off his shirt to reveal his fit salon-tanned upper body and slid down me right off the edge of the bed taking my stretch pants with him.

I lied there in a moistened thong as he knelt at the edge of the bed and resumed his hand stroking of my pussy.

After a few minutes of having me squirming from his hand's delightful massaging, he removed my thong and buried his head between my legs.

I shut my eyes tightly, gripped the sheets and bit hard on my bottom lip. I knew my body very well, its strengths and weakness. What Joseph was about to do was one of my major weaknesses.

He lightly traced the lips of my pussy with his tongue before tugging on each lip with his mouth.

"Whoo,whoo,whoo,whoo", my exhaling began sounding like a choo-choo train going down a railroad track.

He glided his tongue from the bottom all the way up to the top and swirled my inflated clit.

My entire body jerked and shivered as I knew it would, thus the reason for my firm grip on the sheets.

Seeing this, Joseph wrapped his left arm around my right thigh and rested his hand on the skin above my clit and pulled back on it to make the head of my clit peek out.

Just this mere action combined with his blowing air on my clit had a seemingly infinite amount of juices flowing out of me down the crease of my derriere.

Joseph inserted one finger in me and covered my clit with his mouth and began alternating between sucking my clit, flicking it in a circular, side-to-side and up-n-down motion.

"Ahhhhh-Uhnnn, Ooooh-Wooo, AHH, AHH, AHH, AHH, Ooooohhh-SHIT!", I screamed as I began to orgasm out of control.

My eyes were rolled back in my head so far that it was straining the tendon muscles, my stomach contracted faster than a construction jack-hammer and my thighs shook more than a leaf in the middle of hurricane.

Joseph ceased his finger's churning and lifted his head so that he could admire the residual jerking of my orgasm by watching me.

When my eyes finally rolled back down to their normal position, I embarrassedly smiled because I knew that I must've looked crazy during that intense of an orgasm. I wasn't free yet from the after-effect trembling as the coolness of the room's air was reeking havoc on my exposed clit.

Joseph was already better with his mouth than some of the brothas I've had were with their dicks.

Then Joseph made use of the incredible amount of

cream that aligned the insides of my thighs, by using it on his finger that he slid between my derriere cheeks.

The moment his finger began swirling that other hole, my hand rushed to wrap around his wrist.

"Uhn-uhn", I warned Joseph that I didn't do that kind of penetration.

"I'm not going to put it in", he whispered assurance to me as I allowed him to continue tickling that hole.

My lips folded in once again as he resumed tongue-attention on my clit while stimulatingly rubbing his finger across the other hole. Occasionally, the pressure of the finger was in ambiguity territory, not quite qualifying as a penetration, but damn close.

After another bed-shaking orgasm from me, Joseph stood-up and unzipped his pants allowing them to drop to the floor.

I sat forward, grabbed hold of his decent-size 8-incher and started hand stroking it.

"Put your mouth on it", he begged, as I hesitated.

"Do you have a condom?", I asked, as though it was a pre-requisite.

He grabbed one out of the wallet in his pants and opened it faster than a kid opening Christmas presents.

Once the condom was in place, I sucked his thang almost as good as Trina had done to Jamal, if I must say so myself.

"Ahhh, ahhh, ohhh-baby", Joseph groaned.

Several times I think I had him on the verge of cumming, but Joseph being in his early-40's I believed had something to do with his experienced ability to be able to avoid premature ejaculations.

Joseph stood me up, turned me to facing the bed and bent me over.

I knew he would start me off in this position, I thought to myself.

Though he was my first white man, I wasn't surprised that he'd wanna start off in a doggy-style position. I just figured that it was a black-booty thang. He wanted to see mine as he fucked.

What I hadn't expected is for Joseph to be fucking as well as he was. For that matter, the way he was fucking me.

He gripped my butt cheeks with his hands as he pumped and began smacking my ass. That shit was on-point.

During those delicious spanks, I thought about if I ever told Brea about how this white man was handling me, I'd never live it down.

Joseph reached around my waist with his left hand and began rubbing my tender clit while giving me full 8-inch deep strokes. At the same time, with his right hand he'd slid a thumb to tickling that other hole with the same ambiguous pressure of earlier.

His left hands movement made his right-hand temporarily irrelevant to me and Joseph took full advantage by sinking his thumb beyond ambiguity into the realm of my first anal penetration. It wasn't much, an inch-and-a-half or so, but still enough for me not to be able to claim that I hadn't done that.

"Ooooh-ooohhh-ooohhh-wooooah-aaahhH-SHIT! OH SHIT! OH SHIT! OH SHIT!", I cried out at the experience of another enormous orgasm, as I grabbed hold of his clit-stroking left hand.

My knees were jittering inward and I was surprised that his thumb wasn't a discomfort and actually a stimulant.

Growing tired of me being the one worked, I turned more aggressive and pushed Joseph's back to the bed. He just smiled enjoying my playfulness.

I straddled his stomach with my hands on his chest, pinched his nipples 'til I made him have to grab my hands to make me stop.

Reaching behind my butt, I gripped his dick with my hand and gave it a couple of strokes so that it'd regain its hardness and then inserted it in me.

Using my hands on his chest as a solid leverage base, I began dropping down on his dick and rowing my hips.

"Oooo, baby", Joseph uttered at the change of control.

It was me who was in charge of the stimulation and not him.

His eyes began to show how good I was working it by the way they began to close. He grabbed my butt in an effort to diffuse my movements, but I continued dropping deep on him.

"Ooooo, shit, baby. Ahhh, Fff-FUCK!", he moaned urgency of how close he was to orgasm.

I pressed on into high-gear despite that I was also nearing another orgasm from his pubic hair tickling my clit on each grinding stroke.

As a last effort to regain control, Joseph's grip on my butt turned into a pumping finger slid into my ass and I was cumming feverishly, but I was determined that I would make him cum as well.

"Ahhhh, SHIT! I'm GONN---NNN-NNA CUM!", Joseph grunted before I could feel his body gyrating.

I forced my eyes open that had been closed because of the orgasm I was in the middle of, to witness the one I'd created for Joseph.

We just looked at each other with admiration, both our bodies still jerking from our own climax' that our faces couldn't hide.

After a moment of no movement to allow each of us to recover, Joseph pulled me down to him and kissed me on the lips. This time, I returned the kiss.

We layed together for about 20-minutes in each other's arms, before I got cleaned up in the bathroom and tried to restore some order to my hair.

After which, I signed the agreement and went back to my hotel room shortly before midnight.

I hoped that Brea and Trina would be asleep and that I'd be able to slip in undetected so that I wouldn't have to explain what had taken so long or endure a scanning eye of Brea that would uncover even one hair that was out of place.

I wasn't so lucky, as they were both wide-awake as I entered the room.

I gave them the short version of my developmental deal and escaped further scrutiny by claiming to be exhausted and that I'd tell them more in the morning.

Chapter Eight

In the summer after my sophomore year, I still hadn't told my parents about the developmental deal or about my plans to not be returning to Spellman in the fall.

I stayed in touch with my girls by phone. Trina was in Savannah and Brea was back in Brooklyn.

It seemed like there was always something going on with the three of us and uncanny how whenever there was drama, we all had it at the same time.

Trina's parents were considering splitting. At the root of their debate was the fact that Mrs. Whitfield had to spend so much time as a lobbyist up in Atlanta because it was the capital city, Trina explained to me.

Mr. Whitfield had spent years building his car dealership business and was reluctant to move to Atlanta and give that up. Actually he wouldn't be giving it up totally, as he could open a new dealership in Atlanta.

It seemed to me like it was more of a power-struggle between two successful people.

But in either case, it was stressing Trina. She'd even come to stay with me over a weekend just to get away from the arguments that were occurring at home.

It was clear from talking to Brea on the phone that she'd not be returning to Spellman either, due to her loss of an important scholarship. Though she loved Brooklyn, Brea was finding it difficult to accept staying there because of some of the drama that was happening around her. Brea's older brother had just gone to jail on drug charges, her father's shift-hours had been cut in half and money was extremely tight, so she was considering just moving to Atlanta and finding a job.

Simeon and Jamal did open their firm in downtown Atlanta, but Simeon was always very busy traveling to get new accounts so we'd not gotten to kick it in-person as much as I would've liked. However, we talked on the phone a lot.

My dad didn't like Simeon when he visited me at my parent's house. He said it was the age difference, but I paid him no mind for two reasons. One, I was grown and about to turn 21 in July. And two, because to date I've never had a boyfriend that my father did like. All that really mattered was that my mom thought he was a nice and respectful man.

All hell broke loose on the sunny July day that I informed my parents of my plans to pursue a singing career.

I'd told them during my 21st birthday celebration dinner. I know that it was weak to do it on that day, but I'd hoped that it would soften the blow. It did not.

My dad was irate. He went straight ballistic on me.

"What is wrong with you?!", he screamed his disappointment.

My mom made my 16-year old sister, Tyisha and my 12-year old brother, Malcom go to their rooms so not to witness the fireworks.

"I'm 21, now", I said battling back. "It's time for me to make decisions for myself"

"Oh, what? You s'ppose to be grown now?", my dad rhetorically questioned with his finger pointing at me. "You ain't paid a dime of rent in this house! Ain't bought a stitch of clothes that are on your back and ain't put an ounce of food up in that refrigerator, but now you're grown, huh?!"

My mom jumped in trying to slow the onslaught from my dad by softly placing her hand on his forearm to lower his pointing hand away from my face.

"Listen, honey. Jazmyn is grown and is old enough to make her own decisions", my mom defended eventhough I knew she didn't agree with my choice.

"Geraldine, are you trying to defend her?!", my dad turned his attention to my mother.

I felt bad because my mom was undeservingly getting caught in the net of something I created.

"Honey, I'm not saying that I agree with her decision. All's I'm saying is we haven't heard the child-out", mom straddled the negotiator's line impartiality.

"Well as far as I'm concerned, there ain't nothin' to hear-out! She's either going back to Spellman or she's getting out of here. That's it!", my dad spoke, as he made his exit from the kitchen-area dining room into the living room by kicking open the swinging door.

I spent the next few minutes trying to explain my dream and plan to my mother.

"Believe it or not, your father is happy to see you stand-up to him. He'll never show it. But, I'm proud that you feel so strongly about what you want to do. You know that we both love you. Now, I'm not gonna say that I don't wish that you'd change your mind, but you know that I'll support you no matter what. And don't worry about your father. Let me handle that. He'll come around after a little time. He loves you very much and just doesn't wanna see his little girl get hurt", mom calmly explained.

"But I'm not a little girl anymore!"

"I know that and he does too. But to him, you'll always be his little girl. That's just how dads are. You know men ain't got no sense!", she smiled a gender-loyal comment that gained a smile from me, even in the midst of a bad situation.

Two months later, in September, I was moving out of my parents' house and into a small apartment near the AUC (Atlanta University Center) campus. It wasn't much, but that's all that I could afford.

It was a little better than the off-campus housing. A quaint 1-bedroom apartment with an extra room that could be converted to a second bedroom, as Brea was moving back to Atlanta and going to be sharing the $900 a month rent.

Everything was small, the kitchen, the bathroom, the

living room and especially the closets. But for now, it was home.

I liked the location because it was still close to Spellman's campus and my girl, Trina who was the only one of the three of us that was still enrolled in college.

Simeon and Jamal were nice enough to help me move-in what little possessions that I had.

I'd spent most of the $2,000 I'd just received from my developmental deal buying a hooptie car, a 1992 Buick Regal and paying 6-months of auto insurance. After plopping down money on the deposit and paying the first month's rent, including Brea's share because she wasn't in town yet, I had very little left for furnishings. Most of my furniture I bought second-hand at a neighborhood yard-sale, including my sofa and bed. The rest, like pots, pans, dishes, towels, pillows and bed sheets, mom gave to me. The only things that were new were a couple of ghetto-furniture-store-cheap black-n-gold end tables.

By being the first to move-in, I got to choose my bedroom. Of course, I moved my stuff into the large one. The other bedroom wasn't really one at all. It was more like a dining-room that had been converted. It didn't even have a regular door with hinges. Instead it had a pocket-door that slid closed from inside of the wall.

When Brea made it back to Atlanta, I was excited and not just because I was glad that she had the $900 she owed me for her half of the rent and deposit, but it now felt complete.

I'd gotten a job during the summer as a personal trainer at *Run-N-Score* Fitness Club on Stewart Avenue in the East Point Section of Atlanta. The pay wasn't great, but I liked it for two reasons. By working at a gym, it allowed me to keep my body toned and the hours were flexible, which allowed time for me to do some performing in the evening if I ever had a gig.

Run-N-Score was the hood's version of *Bally's*, though the primary focus was basketball, as it had six NBA-size basketball courts, a Barbershop, an Aerobics area and a Free-weights and equipment section.

It could be a bit of a meat-market at times, guys tryin' to mack, but that also made for never having a boring day.

Often, an NBA-player or two would stop-by during the off-season because *Run-N-Score* was known across the country by pro ball-players as a place where they'd be guaranteed to get a good-run. The talent in the pick-up games at the gym was like watching NBA action. High-flying dunks and no-look-behind-the-back passes were ordinary sights.

During the basketball off-season, it was tough for a player to find a place where the competition mirrored the NBA, so many of them utilized *Run-N-Score's* gym to keep their games refined.

Brea was happy to be back in the A-T-L and escape the recent drama of her brother's incarceration. Though she was still upset about it, ironically it was the money that her brother had stashed-away in the house when he was arrested that paid for her move. Her parents didn't want anything to do with the drug money, so she took the 3-grand.

I offered to help her get a job at *Run-N-Score*, but she

declined as she had her own plan as to how she'd get money. Not all of it was on the up-n-up.

Her plan was a combination of dating right and side-hustles like some of the bootleg music and video CDs she'd brought from New York and would sell at beauty salons and nightclubs. I don't know how she got them, but some of CDs she had weren't even available in stores yet.

I didn't like that too much and I could already tell that living with Brea was gonna be much different than just hanging out with her. At the same time, I didn't really care either, I was just glad that she'd have her share of the bills every month, no matter how she got it.

I was anxiously waiting for the month of October to roll around because I was scheduled to fly to New York to perform live for some of the record executives from the label that signed me to the developmental deal. It was a very big deal. This showcase would determine how much interest the label would have in me.

I tried to convince Brea and Trina into forming a trio-group with me, as both of them could sing too. I still felt that I was the best singer, followed by Trina, then Brea. I had visions of Brea choreographing our dance moves for the videos and the three of us becoming the new version of TLC.

Unfortunately, neither of them was as dedicated as I was to the dream and the struggle.

Trina had core-major classes to focus on at Spellman and Brea would be more interested in hooking-up with a star than actually becoming one, which I didn't get.

I think with Brea, she was addicted to the getting-something-for-nothing philosophy. In my mind, I believed she'd actually take less of something she'd gotten free than much more of something she'd have to earn, which made no sense to me, but she was still my girl.

On the second Saturday after Brea moved-in, Simeon and Jamal took me and Brea out to dinner at *Intermezzo*, a hip, trendy and very expensive eatery on Peachtree near the Buckhead-area of Atlanta.

I felt guilty because I'd lied to Trina about my plans for the evening 'cause Brea had never disclosed that she and Jamal were now kickin' it. I just told her that me and Simeon were going to dinner and made no mention of Brea and Jamal.

To be honest, after all this time, I don't think Trina would've cared. But for Brea, I think it was the D.L. thing that fueled her excitement towards Jamal and not a love thang.

Brea had more men than just Jamal interested in her and took full advantage of it.

Having been back less than just 2-weeks, Brea already had many guys calling our house. So much so, I almost hated answering the phone because I knew that it wasn't for me.

"I'll have the lobster tail, ceasar salad, a glass of white wine and a shrimp-cocktail for an appetizer", Brea greedily ordered to the tune of $55 of Jamal's money.

"Damn, girl. You sure can eat to have as nice of a shape like you do!", Jamal shamelessly commented in front of the server at Brea's expensive order.

Brea wasn't fazed by Jamal 'cause I knew the only part of his comment that she heard had to do with her having a nice shape.

Simeon and I just laughed and shook our heads because Brea and Jamal were certainly two of a kind. Both of them were morally-challenged and they knew it about each other, but were still attracted to it nonetheless.

"I'll have the Pasta Linguini with a lemonade", I said, ordering more thoughtfully.

"That sounds good. I'll have the same.", Simeon finished, as the server started collecting our menus.

"Damn, let me see what I can AFFORD to order!", Jamal smiled at Brea who had her head turned to the side and an *I-don't-care* playful smirk on her face. "I'll have the 16-ounce Porterhouse, well done please and a Corona beer".

Judging by Simeon's expression and reactions to Jamal, it was clear that Jamal provided the same entertainment value as Brea did for me. Jamal and Brea were without question the wildest two of the four of us.

Our double-date was strange because it felt like Simeon and I were on our first date and Brea and Jamal were like they'd been married for five years. Both of them felt free to say or do anything they wanted. And often, to me and Simeon's embarrassment, they did.

"How's business going?", Brea asked a general question to both Simeon and Jamal, after our food had arrived.

"Thankfully it's going great!", Jamal returned while swinging a pointing finger at Brea's expensive plate.

I laughed because I knew what he was referring to, that business must be going well for him to be able to afford buying such an expensive meal for Brea.

"Okay. It was funny about the first 10-times, but now it's just getting old. How long are you going to do this?", Brea asked, alluding to his unrelenting teasing of her expensive order.

"I'ma do it about ….. Let me see…..", Jamal said looking up into his head like he was calculating, rubbing his chin and with a smirk on his face, " …. Oh, I'll do it about $55-worth. How's that?"

We all laughed, even Brea broke a grin. Jamal was quick-witted and very funny. He was actually a little faster than Brea, which I didn't think was possible. And I even believe Brea was impressed by it.

During the rest of the dinner conversation, I learned that Jamal was the one who had the actual contacts in the entertainment biz and Simeon had the business strategy and productive planning.

From what I could tell, they seemed to have all areas covered. Jamal's wildness and on-the-prowl style was conducive to attracting clients who were just like him, cocky. And Simeon's discipline and direction guided the business down a prudent path and kept any of Jamal's crazy ideas from sinking the business.

After dinner, we decided to go to Level-3, a downtown nightclub with three floors, hence its name.

It was Reggae-night at the club and the Caribbean music created dé jà vu of the night we'd originally met in Jamaica.

Both Simeon and Jamal were excellent dancers especially to this style of music.

They swung and swayed us all around the dance floor, even spinning us to the opposite partner as me and Brea giggled.

Though they were more mature than us in age by 6-years, we found their playful side to be that much more intriguing.

It'd been a long time since I'd danced with a man that had more endurance than me.

"I need to sit down", I suggested to the pleasure of Brea, the ultimate dancer who was even getting tired.

"What's the matter? Can't hang?", teased Simeon to both of us, as he continued dancing.

"Oh, it's like that?", I playfully returned, surprised by his candid comments.

"Y'all are younger than us and y'all need a break?", added Jamal.

"My feet hurt!", Brea made an excuse. "If y'all had to wear shoes like we do, you wouldn't be talkin' so much shit, either!"

"Uhnnn-hun", Simeon skeptically uttered.

"Ohhhh, I see. Did you hear that Simie? Now, it's the shoes that are the problem", Jamal teased.

Brea hit Jamal across his muscular arm for his latest comment that punched holes in our excuse explaining our lack of stamina.

"C'mon, let's leave them out here to dance with each other", Brea spoke to me as we turned and walked towards a table.

The guys soon caught up to us before we even made it off the dance floor, but not before André, one of the thuggish men Brea knew at the club stopped her to talk.

"Wazzup, Brea? Longtime, no hear", he said facing her directly and getting within two-inches from her face like he owned her.

"Excuse me, paawt-nah!", Jamal said in a male-marking-his-territory deep voice, as he slid his larger frame between him and Brea.

Jamal grabbed Brea by the elbow and escorted her to the table looking directly at the thuggish man the whole time.

A serious-look instantly came across Simeon's face as he guided me into walking ahead of him with a gentle push of his hand on my lower-back. He was making sure to keep his body between me and the thuggish fellow as he also stared at the man as an additional deterrent.

André was a wanna-be-thug, so he did nothing. I knew him from when he used to pick Brea up at Spellman and he just was into playing the part of a thug, but not actually that courageous.

"Who was that Brea?", Jamal asked wanting to know the scoop on possible danger that might be looming.

"He ain't nobody, just some punk-ass nigga I knew when I was at Spellman", she said, waving her hand.

Simeon was staying alert as his head swiveled around the club like a presidential secret-service agent to look for any signs of trouble, as Jamal interrogated Brea.

"André ain't nobody. He just be tryin' to act like he rolls hard. Don't worry about him.", I tried to aid Simeon and Jamal to understanding the situation.

"Oh, ain't nobody worried!", Simeon briefly stopped his surveying head to look me straight in the eye and say.

"Believe dat!", Jamal quickly added in macho-style.

The mood had changed after that incident and Brea and I suggested leaving the club, but we stayed about an hour longer anyway.

I think it was more of a point for Simeon and Jamal to prove to André and any of his boys that they thought might be watching, that they weren't afraid or going to leave because of him.

Me and Brea both mentally gave 'em cool-points for their unwavering defense of us.

Simeon and Jamal regained some of the playfullness of earlier by wrapping their arms around our waists as we were making our way to the exit through a crowd of club-goers that were just entering the club.

What I saw next made my jaw drop. And so did Brea's.

Trina was walking into the club with some friends from Spellman and her eyes widened in disbelief at the sight of Jamal hugged-up behind Brea.

There were no words passed, although I wanted to say something, but didn't know what to say.

Trina just glared at Brea, then me, never even looked at Jamal and then shook her head as the crowd pushed her into the club.

Brea and I just looked at each other.

"Damn", Brea said guilt-ridden as we paused, now on the sidewalk of Peachtree street.

Simeon raised his eyebrows and shook his head in an *I-told-you-so* manner to Jamal.

"C'mon. Let's just go.", Jamal suggested, though he

clearly felt bad.

I thought about going back in to try to explain, but I realized I had no explanation and was just as guilty as Brea for harboring this secret situation from a friend and escalating it by lying to her earlier in the day about where I was going.

I hoped that I'd be able to fix it later, but at that moment, I didn't see how I'd be able to do that.

"Well, there's nothing y'all can do about it right now", Simeon said, recognizing that he was the least guilty of all of us.

He was right, but it was of no real consolation to me.

Chapter Nine

When we returned to Simeon's and Jamal's condo, we watched movies on *HBO*, drank some daiquiris and played Spades.

The uncomfortable moment at the club had not been erased, but no one made it a subject and after a few daiquiris there was little, if any residue left.

After we lost several games, due mostly to Brea's overbidding, she blurted out an idea.

"I don't like this game. Besides, I play much better when there's something at stake!", she challenged.

"Tell me anything. We'll beat you at any game. You name the game.", Jamal said, up for the challenge.

"Let's play 21.", Brea suggested.

"Girl, please. I play in Las Vegas, twice a year, you better pick a different game if you want any chance of winning", Jamal aggressively warned.

"I'on't care about no Vegas. The game is 21. Strip-21", Brea said, waiting to see if he'd chicken out.

I was trippin' that she'd suggested that, but nothing was ever a total shock from Brea.

I looked at Simeon who didn't seem to be too bothered, but didn't wanna give away to me, whether or not he was a clear supporter of the suggested game. His face was expressionless as he glanced at me.

I was a little uncomfortable at the possibility of Brea and I losing, but also stimulatingly intrigued at the sensual idea.

Realistically, I think Simeon and I were both sort-of down for playing the game but didn't know what each other would think if we were obvious about it.

Before I could make a comment, the first hand was already being dealt by Jamal.

Because only two hands were dealt, it was clear that we were playing as teams.

Jamal had a 4 showing and the other card was face-down, so we couldn't see it because he was the dealer on this hand.

Brea and I had a Jack and a 6, for a total of 16.

"Hit me!", Brea said, without consulting with me first.

As Jamal turned over our hit-card, which was an 8 that caused us to be busted, I smacked Brea on the arm.

"Wait for me on the next hand!", I yelled at Brea.

"Jaz, we had 16, you never hold at 16!", she tried to

defend her play.

We were playing for clothes, so I wanted to at least think about it first and didn't appreciate her controlling what play we'd make on her own.

"Brea, maybe I wanted to stay at sixteen and see if they'd be busted. You never know!", I scolded further.

"Whatevah", Brea spewed.

The argument was point-less 'cause it didn't change the fact that we'd lost the first hand and had to strip.

"Yee-aaahhh", Jamal said rubbing his hands together like an evil scientist in anticipation of the removal of our first garment.

I was glad that I had on a bra, as I took off my top. Brea didn't have one on, but didn't seem to care about her bare breast exposure, even in the presence of Simeon as she without hesitation quickly pulled her top over her head and was anxious to even the score.

I also saw Jamal not so subtly checking me out too, as his face showed disappointment that I wasn't bare-breasted like Brea, who he'd already seen naked in Jamaica.

Simeon actually seemed more uncomfortable than Brea as he tried to play-it-off by not allowing his eyes to be drawn to where I know they wanted to go, Brea's big-ass-titties. He stared at me, Jamal and the cards, but I could tell from my peripheral vision that when I looked down at the new hand that Brea dealt, his eyes seized the opportunity to glare at her breasts.

Simeon and Jamal had a 9 and an 8 for a total of 17. We had a 10 showing and our face-down card was another 10 for a total of 20.

The only way they could win this hand was to get to

21. Though the odds were in our favor, my heart was still racing because it was Strip-21.

Brea and I didn't show in our faces of how good our hand was because if they didn't take a hit, we'd already won.

"Do you want a hit?", Brea asked coyly as Jamal intensely tried to read her face.

They pondered and talked about it for a few seconds while looking at us to try to determine what our face-down card was.

"No", Jamal finally said, as Brea and I released face-stretching grins as we turned over our cards to show that we'd won.

Brea mimicked Jamal by rubbing her hands together as they removed their shirts.

The next hand we won automatically, as Jamal dealt us a blackjack hand.

"I don't hear you talkin'", Brea taunted Jamal's earlier claim of superiority in this game.

We reveled as we watched them strip-down to just their underwear and the excitement of being only one-hand away from winning it all.

Adding to the enthusiasm was that we were the dealers in the next hand, which was an advantage because they'd have to take a hit first and not know our face-down card.

Butterflies were in my stomach as I dealt this hand.

Simeon and Jamal had two 8's for a total of 16. We had a 6-showing and 7 that was face-down for a total of 13.

My nervousness increased because I figured that Simeon and Jamal would not take a hit and risk getting busted, especially when they only had underwear left as clothing. That would mean that we'd have to take a hit and could lose.

To my surprise, they took the risk.

"Hit me", Jamal spoke, but not confidently.

"Dammmmmmnnn!", Brea and I shouted as we saw the 4 that gave them a total of 20.

"Yeah! Yeah! Yeah!", Jamal and Simeon grunted like they'd just made a last-second shot in a basketball game.

We had no choice, we had to go for 21.

Our first card was a 6, which added to our 13 gave us 19.

"C'mon two! C'mon two!", Brea begged the deck of cards.

"Awww, HELL NAW!", Simeon and Jamal screamed at the sight of the 2 that Brea'd pleaded the deck to provide.

We'd won the hand!

Brea's ass was so excited that she'd jumped up out of the chair in victory to high-five me, without consideration to her bra-less state.

That moment of Brea's absent-mindedness seemed to briefly heal the wound of defeat for Simeon and Jamal, as they both attentively gawked at Brea's bouncing breasts.

"STRIP! STRIP!", Brea pointed a command to both of them with one hand as she used the other to fold across her chest and stop her titties from bouncing.

Simeon and Jamal honored their defeat by shedding

their briefs, as Brea's scandalous ass actually walked around the table to get a better view.

Simeon had returned to sitting after removing his underwear, but not before I'd gotten a chance to see that he had a potential 12-incher himself.

Mmmmpphh!, I thought to myself, yet cautious to not be as damn bold as Brea.

"Alright, you won, now what's up?!", Jamal said standing up with his 12-incher dangling and beginning to get hard.

I sat back down by Simeon as we watched Brea's ass stare directly at Jamal as she walked right up to him and tightly grab hold of his thang while tip-toe-ing to kiss him.

They were so wild it made for an uncomfortable moment for me and Simeon.

Number one, we weren't as out-going as they were and didn't want to start doing something just because Brea and Jamal were, like we're their younger siblings or something.

The speed of the moment had caught us off-guard that neither one of us knew no way out of it.

When Brea knelt before Jamal and began sucking on his dick, Jamal looked over at us.

"What's up y'all?!", Jamal urged us to get busy doing something.

"I got this!", Simeon defended the moment and me. "Handle yo' business!".

Brea briefly paused her dick-sucking to look back at me with an eyebrow-raising expression, as if to say that I should do something with Simeon.

Though I could see that Simeon's dick was rising, he chose to be more sophisticated and treat me with more respect than his orgy-esque partner. He opened his arm and invited me to lean into a cuddle with him.

I laid the left-side of my head on his chest and rubbed my right hand on his ripped stomach.

I was horny and very attracted to Simeon, but if something was going to happen, I wasn't down for making it an exhibition like Jamal and Brea were doing right now.

First of all, I actually cared about Simeon, unlike the two of them. Brea had other men and I'm sure the same was true for playboy-Jamal. Not to mention that my first-time, or that matter anytime with Simeon was not gonna be on display.

"Awww, awww, awww, ohhh-wah, OHHH-WAH", I could hear Brea moaning as I peered at her with my right eye and avoiding moving my head from Simeon's chest, so not to make him aware that I was looking at them.

I'm sure he was doing the same because he was very still. Too still, except for his hightened breathing.

Brea was on her back, squeezing her own titties in her hands while licking her own nipples, made solely possible because of her well-endowment. Her back was arched and her head jerking up-n-down as Jamal was eating her pussy and fingering her at the same time.

"Oh shit, baby. OH, Shit, Baby. OHHH, SHEE-IT BABY! ", Brea screamed at the top of her lungs.

Her hands fell from her breasts to the floor trying to grip the carpet as her head rose.

Jamal's face was as fiercely focused on Brea's face as

her eyes disappeared in the top of her half-open eyelids and her entire body began doing the orgasm dance.

"Ighh, cummm ... mmm-nnnen, Iiigh... mmm ... kahhh ... minnn ... nnen", Brea's voice stuttered from the vibration of her body's quake.

At that point, I'd seen enough. Well actually, I felt that Simeon had seen enough. I began putting my top back on and Simeon did the same with his clothes without my urging.

We decided to leave them alone in the condo. I couldn't believe how oblivious they were able to be as we walked past them to get to the door. Jamal was gripping Brea's ass and rhythmically doggy-styling her just like we weren't even walking by. Didn't even stop for a moment.

As I followed behind Simeon, I couldn't resist one last glance. Jamal had a seriously determined look on his face and was biting his bottom lip just before he gave Brea the first in a series of three very powerful, butt-shaking 10-inch deep strokes that raised Brea's slumped head to reveal a weary, furrowed-brow, squint-faced and rounded-lip expression she had.

"Ohhhhhh!, Ohhhhh!, Ohhhhhh!", she grunted in tune with each stroke, which almost made it tough for me to close the door behind me.

Brea's about to get her ass worn the fuck out!, I thought to myself.

Instinctively, I felt some concern for her. Just reflex, I guess, especially after seeing the last face she'd made. But I eased my worry by knowing that she'd fucked him before, so she should know the deal.

We got into Simeon's Range Rover and drove to get

something to eat at IHOP and to allow Jamal and Brea to finish-up. It was either that or Waffle House and I never liked the Waffle House's clientele this late at night.

"I'm sorry about that", Simeon apologized to me unnecessarily.

"Don't worry about it. It's no big deal. And, it's not your fault!", I said, but feeling guilty because I wasn't that bothered by the action. In fact, my nipples still hadn't softened yet.

I felt like I should be apologizing to him. I saw how hard his dick had gotten watching Brea. I know he wanted or needed some sex. Even thought about having him take us back to my apartment, but I didn't wanna make the first move.

When we returned, we sat in the car in the parking lot and kissed for awhile. I felt like a teenager again. Simeon caressed my body with his hands, my hips, my legs, my butt and finally gave my breasts the physical reason to be perky.

Just great! Now he makes a move on me!, I thought to myself.

If it had been earlier, we could've done something about it. But now it was nearly 5:00 AM and I wasn't sure if Brea wanted to stay at Simeon's and Jamal's condo all night.

For me to take Simeon home now would mean that I wouldn't be back until probably 11:00 AM. Our apartment was a good 30-minute drive from theirs. I had my car keys in my purse, plus I didn't want Brea driving my car anyway, as high as my insurance was already.

I certainly hoped that sex with Simeon would last longer than the roundtrip travel time, so it was clear that it was just too late for that.

Most importantly, I didn't want rushed sex with Simeon. I dug him. I wanted it to mean more, for him and for me.

As we entered the condo, Jamal and Brea had already showered and gotten dressed. They were relaxing in a cuddle on the sofa.

I was just glad to see that Brea was still alive because of the way she looked when we'd left.

"Are you ready to go?", I asked Brea.

"Yeah, when-ever?", she calmly responded.

She got up and leaned over to give Jamal, who didn't even bother to walk her to the door, a good-bye kiss.

Simeon gave me an *I-wish-you-didn't-have-to-go* goodbye hug and tongue-kiss that made sure that I'd end-up dreaming about him all night.

In the car, an exhausted Brea was curled-up in the passenger seat, semi-asleep. I didn't want to wake her, but I was tired too and doing the driving.

"Brea. Brea.", I called her name.

"Yeah, Jaz.", she answered with her eyes still closed.

"So what's the deal with you and Jamal?", I couldn't help but ask.

"What'dya mean?"

"I mean, what's the deal with you and Jamal?", I repeated my already clear-enough question.

"Ain't nothin'. We're just kickin' it", she made light of their relationship.

"You mean we done fucked up with Trina and y'all just kickin' it?", I questioned.

Brea opened her eyes and turned my direction to look at me.

"I know -- it's messed-up with Trina right now. But, we'll be girls again", she tried to convince me.

"I don't think that you get it. Trina might never speak to us again!"

"Quit trippin'! Of course she will. It just might take a little time. I mean, when you really think about it, what did I do that was so wrong?"

"Did you just say 'what did you do that was so wrong?' You mean like lying to one of your best friends, doesn't count? How 'bout fucking your best friend's....umm...ummm...."

"See there it is right there. What is Jamal to her? It ain't like he was her man or nothin'!"

"Okay, now you're trippin'! That's just a ghetto-technicality", I attempted to bring Brea back to reality.

"The way I see it, actually, I kinda did her a favor."

"A what??!"

"A favor. She might've thought that Jamal would've been loyal to her, but now she knows better", Brea tried to place a silver-lining in a very black cloud.

"Brea, I think you should've been a Political Science major at Spellman, 'cause that's bullshit and you know it!"

"You know what your problem is?"

"What? Listening to you? Or lying for you?", I snapped back.

"Neither. Your problem is that you're always thinking about what bad can happen instead of living in the moment and going after what you want"

"Now how did I become the subject all of a sudden?"

"No, I'm serious. You're always thinking about what your parents are going to say and about the possible bad side of any situation. You never spend as much time thinking about the good that can come out of a situation"

Brea was hitting home with me, but I wasn't gonna let her escape that easily from blame of her wrong-doing of Trina or convince me that I somehow shouldn't be feeling guilty like I deserved.

"You don't even know what you're talking about!", I responded.

"Yes I do. Like tonight, for example"

"What about tonight?", I challenged.

"Simeon was diggin' you and I know you were diggin' him. There he was, butt-naked and you didn't fuck him and I know that you wanted to!"

"Just 'cause I ain't no damn freak like you....."

"Freak ain't got shit to do with it! You wouldn't even know if you were a freak or not because you always think too much! You and Trina are a lot alike, sometimes."

"You mean, 'cause we care about someone other than ourselves every once in awhile?"

"You can get it twisted if you want, but you know what I mean. So, let's use tonight as an example. Let's say that there were other women playing Strip-21. While yo' ass is thinking about the consequences of what Simeon might think, some other woman acts on her urges and goes to get her freak-on with Simeon, would you blame her?"

"No. I'd blame him, if he wanted that hoe!"

"I'll ignore that you're calling me a hoe, because that's

what I did with Jamal. And by the way, you just proved my point that I really did nothing wrong by kicking it with Jamal"

"I didn't say that! Now you're trying to twist stuff. The difference from that example you gave and the truth is that you're s'pposed to be Trina's friend and in your example the girl did it in front of my face", I countered.

"Now you're talkin' technicalities. I still love ya. Yo' ass just need a good fucking, that's all"

"Bitch, please. You don't know what I need!"

"That's all you need and you'll be alright"

It was a low-blow and pissed me off because I think she was partially right. But I hated that she was sure that she was. So, I attempted to return my own low-blow.

"Ohhh and I guess you got yours tonight, huh?"

"Damn right I did!", she bragged.

"That's not the way I saw it. As much shit as you talk, you didn't seem to be doing much better than Trina with Jamal like you said you would in Jamaica! Remember this, *'I'd have that nigga cumming all the way down the hallway'*. Remember that?", I mockingly repeated her quote from Jamaica. "Jamal had you're ass screaming, crying and begging like a 12-year old girl when I left!"

My comments had their desired effect as Brea was upset that I was making fun of her.

"You don't know what the fuck you're talking about!"

"If you can't take the heat.......", I mercilessly continued jabbing at her.

"Jaz, U don't even know what you're talking about!"

It's you that can't handle a big-dick nigga like Jamal or Simeon! That's probably why you didn't wanna fuck Simeon, 'cause you don't even know what to do"

"And you do?", I said quickly, actually too quickly as I semi-admitted that I didn't know what to do.

"Hell yeah! If you shut-up and listen, maybe you can learn a thing or two!"

"Go ahead Miss Big-Dick Queen, I'm listening", I said.

"See, you playin' and I'm for real. Yeah Jamal has a big dick and knows how to work that shit, I'll give you that. But, I could've stopped it at anytime. If you had stayed you would've learned how to make a nigga like that cum when you need him to!"

I thought Brea might be bullshitting me to cover how Jamal was wearing her ass out, but I was intrigued as to what she meant because I couldn't put it passed her that she might know some secret sex tricks. Still, I played it off by acting as though she was gonna tell me something I already knew.

"I'm listening?", I said trying not to show how interested I really was.

"Alright, with a big-dick nigga that can have your ass orgasm-ing for a month if you let him, when you feel that you're about to lose all control, all you have to do is get him to fuck you in the missionary position. Before you go into a deep orgasm and lose control of your body, as he's pumping you, slide a finger deep into his asshole. You'll be trippin' how even the biggest-dick niggas cum immediately! That's what I did to Jamal, tonight! I had his eyes rolling around in his head and his voice sounding like he was the woman as he came for about 2-minutes straight!", she boasted.

"Dayyyummm!", I said at her revelation, having forgotten that we were previously in the midst of an argument.

"I'm telling you, it works every time!", she assured. "You see what I'm saying? You run from things when you actually have a way to handle them. You just don't know it because you're always too damn busy running".

As we pulled into the parking lot of our apartment, ironically, I did see her point. But, I still didn't agree about what we'd done to Trina.

"I hear you, but you know we're wrong, maybe not for the 'what' we did to Trina, but how we did it. We should've just been straight with her", I said.

"That's all I'm saying. You're right, we should've told her, and then she couldn't blame me because Jamal liked me. Well, there's only two things that can happen now", Brea semi-agreed.

"What's that?"

"She'll either forgive us or she won't"

Brea spoke the truth. There was no sense in fearing the outcome as she made me recognize that I normally did. That was needless, as whether I worried or not, there would still remain only those two options.

Chapter Ten

In late October, I was packed and running late to the Hartsfield International Airport to catch my flight to New York City to sing for all of the record label executives.

Neither Brea nor I had spoken to Trina. Well, Trina hadn't spoken to us. We'd left messages at the dorm for her, but she never answered any of our calls.

When we finally decided to go by her dorm, we found that she didn't live there anymore as her parents had made the move from Savannah to Atlanta and Trina lived at their new suburban home in Alpharetta, Georgia.

Brea was dropping me off at the airport and I hoped that I wouldn't regret allowing her to use my car while I was in New York for three days.

She needed my car because she had tried-out for and

made the Atlanta Hawks cheerleading team. The job didn't pay hardly anything, only $75 per game and a pair of prime-seating tickets. But that didn't matter to Brea, she was all about the shine anyway. It was more about the fact that she was one of only 16-women that made it, out of over 1,200 that tried-out.

Her real job, well the way she made the rent money was still from selling her bootleg CDs and DVDs at the clubs and beauty salons. And of course, some of the revenue she got from the plethora of men that she dated.

I think being a part of the Atlanta Hawks cheerleading squad was just another magnet for her to use to intrigue more fellas by telling them she was a part of the team.

When I arrived at NYC's JFK Airport, the record label had a car waiting for me to take me to my hotel.

As I went to the baggage claim area, I saw a limo driver holding a sign with my name on it.

"Hi, I'm Jazmyn Wallace", I said to the man.

"Welcome to New York, Ms. Wallace. My name is Curtis, I'll be your driver while you're in town."

"Ohhhh-kaayyy?", I said sounding like a rookie, but lovin' every moment of it.

"If you'll be so kind as to point-out your bags, I'll be happy to collect them for you and put them in the car", Curtis said courteously.

After he'd put them in the jet-black Lincoln Towncar,

I didn't know what I was suppose to do, so I offered him cash as a tip.

"Oh, thank you, but I can't accept it. Everything has been taken care of for me.", he said.

I wonder if I was looking stupid to Curtis by not knowing the protocol. But Curtis seemed to be on my side by not making me feel bad about being in awe. He was black and in his late-20's or early-30's, so that helped.

"Just relax Ms. Wallace. The entire weekend, I'll take care of everything for you!"

"I appreciate it Curtis. Listen, you don't have to call me Ms. Wallace, you can call me Jazmyn", I offered to my new friend.

"Well, they like me to use a sir-name with clients", he explained.

"I won't tell, if you won't?", I smiled to him in the rear view mirror.

"Alright, cool Jazmyn", he said returning his own smile.

As we pulled into the luxurious entrance of The Plaza Hotel on Fifth Avenue in Manhattan near Central Park, my eyes widened and I wished that I had someone to share it with.

"Here we are, The Plaza Hotel", Curtis said after opening my door for me.

"Thank you.", I returned in a daze, busy looking around.

"You're already checked-in. Here are your room keys, Ms. Wallace and my card. Call me if you ever need to go anywhere, I'm on call 24-hours a day the entire weekend for you", Curtis said, as I was nervous about his departure.

The bellhops moved like I was a superstar unloading my bags from the limo onto a brass cart and whisking them up to my room.

"Umm, Curtis?....", I began speaking from fear of not knowing the ropes in this situation.

"Don't worry, Jazmyn...", Curtis leaned over to whisper advice, "...you'll be fine. You don't have to pay for anything, no tipping at all. I'll be in room 2504, if you need me. Or just call me, okay?"

"Listen. Curtis. Do you mind keeping me company for a while?", I asked, apparently too loudly, as Curtis *shhhhush'd* me with his finger pressed to his lips.

"No problem, Jazmyn. I'm really not supposed to do that, but I'll meet you at your suite", he assured me.

As I looked down at my card key to find what room I was in, Curtis told me that he already knew it, but for appearance-sake wanted to meet me there rather than walking to it together.

One of the bellhops led me to the elevator and directed me to the incredibly spacious 2760-square foot Astor Suite. It was larger than my parents' house, complete with 3-bedrooms, a huge living room, Crystal chandelier, Flat-screen TV's, a dining room that sat 10-people, Marble floors and Fireplace, a Jucuzzi with a view of Central Park and a King-size canopy bed in the Master bedroom.

I couldn't believe where I was, it was some shit that be on MTV Cribs.

I'd just whipped out my camera and was about to call Brea, when I heard a knock on the door. I put away my camera because I thought it might be some of the executives from the record-company. It was Curtis.

"How do you like the suite?", Curtis asked with a smile enjoying reading my eyes.

"Are you kidding me? I love it. I see there are 3-bedrooms, are there going to be other singers staying here too?", I innocently asked.

Curtis couldn't contain his laughter.

"No sweetheart. This is all for you", he said.

I couldn't believe it, but I was glad that I had Curtis around so that I didn't have to front and could be myself.

Curtis spent the next few minutes as my personal photographer taking pictures of me in every inch of the hotel room until we'd used all four rolls of the disposal cameras I'd brought.

"Don't worry, I'll get you some more cameras", Curtis offered, as he headed towards the door on his way to the gift-shop downstairs.

"Hey, umm, Curtis?", I said before he left.

"Yes, Jazmyn?", he said holding the door open and turning around.

"Ummm. Thanks, man!", I said sincerely, referring to his willingness to make me more comfortable and not just simply for the camera-errand.

He smiled a gorgeous grin before saying, "It's my pleasure, Jazmyn" and then left.

I think Curtis also appreciated the fact that I wasn't the norm for him either. I'm sure that in his job he's had his share of ego-driven, spoiled entertainers.

While Curtis was gone, I jumped on my cell phone with Brea.

"Gurrlll, I'm telling you, this place is the shit!", I

exclaimed.

"See, I knew I should've come with you!", Brea said disappointed that she'd chosen to stay because she'd lose her spot on the Atlanta Hawks cheerleading team if she missed a game.

"Yeah, I think I may take a Jucuzzi later and have a little wine before watching a movie on my Flat-screen", I playfully said in a Royal-English accent.

"Jaz, you ballin'!! I know you're gonna take pictures", Brea said wishing she could see them right now.

"Brea, I done already taken four rolls!"

Brea laughed, as the phone in my room began to ring.

"Gurl, that's the phone. It might be the record-label execs, I gotta call you back", I said, as I rushed to get off the phone with her and raced to the hotel phone.

"Hello?"

"Hi, Jazmyn, it's Joseph. I see that you made it. How's everything?"

"Oohh, it's great! Fantastic!"

"I was just calling to welcome you. Have fun, go sight-seeing or whatever you want to do and we'll see you tomorrow at the studio. Curtis should be taking care of everything for you"

"Curtis is great!", I said trying to put in a good word for him.

"That's good to hear. Be rested for tomorrow, we've got a busy day, but have fun too, okay?"

"I'll be ready!", I made sure to make him aware that I wasn't gonna just kick it and forget the reason that I was here in the first place.

Curtis returned with 10 more cameras. I laughed because he'd gotten so many and because he knew damn well that I planned to use every shot in each of them before I left New York.

"I just got off the phone with Joseph Myers. He said that I'm free today and don't have to go to the studio until tomorrow"

"Oh, yeah. I'm sorry, I have your itinerary right here, I forgot to give it to you", Curtis said with concern.

"Oh, it's no problem!", I said trying to ease his concern. "I told Joseph that you've been great!"

"Thanks. I appreciate that!"

"If you're not busy, I wondered if you'd mind showing me some sights?", I asked.

He laughed yet again at me before saying, "That's my job. What did you want to see?"

"I didn't mean it like that. I don't want to feel like I'm bossing you around. I meant, would you mind going sight-seeing WITH me, not as your job?", I asked.

"Sure. Let me get the car"

Even when Curtis had gotten the car, I had to allow him to open the back door just in case someone was looking. After we'd driven a couple of blocks from the hotel, I climbed over the front seat so that I could sit next to him instead of feeling like some obnoxious aristocrat in the backseat.

"You are a trip!", Curtis relaxed.

"Why? 'Cause I ain't all boogee?", I asked.

"Jazmyn, you're cool with me! I like ya", he smiled which made me smile too.

133

"Where we going?", I questioned.

"Harlem. 125th Street. We can drive by the Cotton Club and the Apollo Theatre"

"Cool!"

I loved the tour Curtis gave. It was more than the typical sight-seeing tour of what you'd see on Seinfeld re-runs. It was more of a real tour, with real people. I called it my hood tour. 125th Street in Harlem, Fordham Road in the Bronx, Jamaica Ave in Queens and Flatbush Ave in Brooklyn, of which I'd heard so much about from Brea.

We did drive by places like Yankee Stadium and checked-out all the lights in Times Square later in the evening, too.

It was a little after 9:00 PM when we arrived back at The Plaza, I'd already climbed back into the backseat, so that Curtis could appear to others to be doing his job by opening the door for me and not having me in the front seat.

"Meet me at my room", I whispered to Curtis as he opened the door and addressed me as Ms. Wallace.

He nodded that he would.

I could really relate to Curtis because the only reason he was staying at such a posh hotel was because he was on-duty, which was reminiscent of me cleaning houses for my family business while dreaming that I lived in them.

Though the hotel suite was cool, it was so large that being in it by myself felt lonely.

I was glad to see Curtis when he arrived shortly after parking the car.

"Wassup! Wassup!", Curtis greeted me much differently than earlier in the day.

"Nothing", I sung back to him.

He was still in his black suit uniform and tie. I'd already changed into some jean shorts and a white muscle-shirt tank top.

"Curtis, do you have any other clothes with you?", I asked, wanting him to feel comfortable.

"Yeah, I do in my room downstairs", he said, glad that I asked.

"I ain't going nowhere else tonight. You can go change and come back up. Maybe we'll watch a movie or something?"

"Cool! You ain't gotta tell me twice!"

It was 30-minutes later before he came back. I'd just started to worry about whether or not he'd gone to sleep or something. I didn't wanna call him, just in case he had gone to sleep, 'cause I'd look just like one of those bothersome entertainers that I figured he was use to.

"What took you so long?", I asked.

"I decided to take a shower, too"

Curtis was looking much better than he did in that limo-driver outfit. Now he had on a pair of jeans, some Timberlands and a Malcom-X t-shirt that was stylishly tucked in the front of his pants with the tail of the shirt hanging-out on the sides and the back.

I also noticed he'd put in an earring in his left ear and smelled delicious.

Even the swagger in his step matched his ensemble as he made his way to the sofa.

"Alright, what'dya wanna watch? *'Training Day'* with

Denzel Washington or *'Monster's Ball'* with Halle Berry?", I asked.

"'*Monster's Baller'* is cool", he said innocently.

"Ummm-hmmm. I'll bet!", I smirked to him at his preference because that movie had a nude scene in it.

"Actually, it don't matter to me. I like 'em both.", he tried to disguise the reason for his choice.

"Naw, don't change your mind now. We'll watch *'Monster's Ball'*", I agreed.

Before the movie began, I went to the bar to get a glass of wine.

"Curtis, did you want a beer or something?", I asked.

He hesitated for a moment because he was technically on-duty and wasn't supposed to be drinking. He knew that I said that I wasn't going anywhere else tonight, but still wanted to not have one of the Label Execs drop-by unexpectedly and find him with beer on his breath. After much convincing that it was too late for a visit from a Label Exec, he finally accepted a beer.

We sat next to each other on the sofa like co-workers and talked 20-minutes into the movie before I thought about my late-night, drive-home conversation with Brea from a month ago.

Reaching behind me, I grabbed one of the sofa cushions, as Curtis looked at me with curiosity.

"Excuse me. Do you mind?", I said, as I placed the cushion in his lap, slid me feet from the floor to the sofa and laid my head on the cushion to get ultra comfortable.

Curtis smiled looking down at me as his right hand cautiously glided through my hair.

"That feels good!", I interjected at the very moment of his first touching of my scalp trying to encourage him to continue.

Curtis' left hand ran so smoothly up and down my arm it created goose-bumps. The combination of his hair and tingling arm massage made my nipples pierce my white muscle-shirt tank top, but I didn't care. Didn't cover 'em with my arms or get a blanket to hide 'em. I was determined to remain secure in my body.

Handsome men caressing your body makes your nipples get hard, that's natural!, I reaffirmed in my head to keep me from giving in to inhibitions.

Curtis never attempted to over-step boundaries and soon I'd drifted asleep in his arms.

In the morning, I sprung awake scared that I'd over-slept and disoriented because I was lying in the bed.

My mind struggled to try to recap last night and how I'd gotten in the bed.

I lifted the sheets to look under them to see what I had on.

"Whew!!!", I exhaled relief that I still had on the same shorts and the t-shirt from last night. Fueling more relief was that my t-shirt was still tucked into my shorts.

I wasn't sure if Curtis was still in the suite or not. Looking at the unfettered sheets on the left side of the bed, I knew that he'd not slept next to me.

I went to the living room and didn't see him at all.

"Curtis? Curtis?", I beckoned for him a couple of times before noticing a note propped up on the cocktail table.

I began reading the note.

Enjoyed last night! You're a sweet lady. Figured you needed your rest for a big day today, so I couldn't leave you on the sofa. Hope you don't mind?? Call me whenever you're ready. C.

I smiled because he was so thoughtful that he must've carried me to the bedroom and honorable enough not to take advantage of my tired state.

I looked at the clock and it was just 7:45 AM. His note made me want to call him right then, but I didn't have to be at the studio until Noon, so I didn't wanna wake him.

I formulated an excuse and called anyway.

"Hello.", Curtis answered wide-awake.

"Hi, Curtis, it's Jazmyn. I got your note."

"I hope you didn't mind me carrying you to your bed, I just wanted you to get a good night's rest, that's all", he cutely explained, which had me blushing laughter.

"No, I don't mind. Thank you. I just hope you didn't hurt your back carrying me"

"No chance of that, you're as light as a feather!", he complimented so sweetly that it guaranteed that my day was gonna need to start with a cold shower.

"Did you want to get some breakfast?"

"Sure. What time?"

"You tell me. I just woke-up and could be ready in 45-minutes"

"So, I'll come get you at your suite at 8:30 AM, is that cool?"

"I'll be ready!", I spoke cheerfully.

When Curtis arrived, he was dressed in uniform and I wished that he didn't have to wear it or that I had the power to say that it was okay for him not to wear it. But I did realize that this was his job and being spotted without it could get him fired, no matter what I said to defend him.

When we arrived at the studio, I was introduced to the Label Executives and the rest of the Management Team by Joseph Myers. He'd ushered me from the limo so fast I'd not even had the chance to give a proper good-bye to Curtis who had to remain behind and wasn't permitted to come inside. I looked over my shoulder as Joseph was hurriedly guiding me along with a hand in the middle of my back.

Curtis signaled good-luck to me with a smile and a thumbs-up gesture and his eyes communicated that he understood that I wasn't being rude by not properly saying good-bye.

The staff rushed me through a tour of the office like it was the Indy 500. We passed through hallways with Platinum-Record plaques on the wall and peaked in offices for abbreviated introductions. I couldn't believe how busy the office was and it was a Saturday, but I guess the music industry has different hours.

Eventually we ended-up in a large conference room with a mahogany-wood oval-shaped table that sat 20-people.

Also in the room was a mini stage, complete with a sophisticated lighting system, state-of-the-art speakers and musical equipment.

I felt like a piece of meat as the movers-and-shakers appeared to be looking me over.

I was the only one on my side of the table and there were 12 of them on the other side.

They began the meeting in an informal fashion like we were just talking, but it was uncomfortable because I was the sole subject.

Everything was fair game for them to ask. My ethnic background, age, sexual preference, if I'd ever done nude modeling, used drugs, worked at a strip-club, done porn movies, was I into devil-worship-ing, did I have children -- you name it, they asked it.

Joseph tried to cushion the questions by making it clear that they may choose to invest a lot of money in me and that they were just trying to make sure there would be no surprises that would affect my public image, thereby affecting their investment.

While I understood that, it made their interrogation no less uncomfortable.

After the interview, which lasted an hour, I went to wardrobe to get my measurements taken and was given a brand new tiny bikini to put on and wear back into the room. The bikini was so small it covered little more than my nipples, my coochie and just barely the crack of my ass.

As I timidly entered the room of fully-clothed white executives, they were being handed a newly-copied stat-sheet of my measurements.

It made me feel as though I was a slave being paraded on the auction block. They asked me to turn around so they could view all of me and to mimic poses that were in recent glamour fashion magazines that they'd placed on the table in front of me.

All in all, they seemed professional about it. No one was gawking or trying to get turned on by making me model. They were simply trying to get an idea of what type of promotional shoots I could and couldn't do.

A photographer was busy taking pictures of each pose, so that they could review and remember them later. And the wardrobe designer was holding big swatches of different color pastel fabric in front of my chest to see which colors went best with my facial complexion.

As if that weren't enough stress, sometimes they even candidly spoke about me like I wasn't even in the room.

"She's gotta nice shape, but she doesn't quite have that Beyoncé or J.Lo booty and her breasts may be a little too small", spoke Emily, one of the Marketing Execs in her mid-40's.

My breasts are too small for who or for what? And I know ain't nothing wrong with my butt!, I wanted to say to that white bitch.

"No, Emily look at her, she's gorgeous! Think about Ashanti when you look at her. She's got a sexy-style about her that overcomes the lack of any one attention-getting body component", defended Jeff, another one of the Marketing Execs, who was flamingly gay.

Uncomfortably listening to them debate my physical attributes I asked, "Do you still need me to stand here? Or can I go change?"

"Hang on just a few more minutes, Jazmyn. I know it's tough to hear this, but be strong!", Joseph intervened and encouraged.

I'd heard that you have to possess thick-skin to make

it in the music business, but I didn't know that it'd have to be whale-blubber-thick, because this was almost unbearable.

"I'm just skeptical because she doesn't look very comfortable with her sexuality. Look how awkward she looks", Emily continued arguing with Jeff.

"I'm very comfortable with my sexuality!", I said unable to take anymore.

"Jazmyn.....wait....", Joseph tried to stop me.

"Uhn-un, Joseph. I've stood here and listened to her talk about that my titties are too small and my ass ain't big enough.", I spoke in Brea-like style with one-hand-palm-facing-her gestures.

"Umm, Jazmyn...", Joseph again attempted to interrupt.

"No let her continue", Emily suggested to Joseph.

"I like my titties! And contrary to what you might think, they're just the right size. Besides, any more than a mouthful is just a waste!", I added by gripping them in my hands. "And as far as my butt is concerned, I ain't never had N-E complaints from N-E man! So you can say what you want, do what you want, but I know I can sing and nobody's gonna tell me that I ain't sexy-enough to sell records!"

"Are you finished?", Emily asked snidely.

"R-U?", I returned, as I saw Joseph's shoulders moved up and down from his laughing at my sistah-girl rampage.

"Okay, okay. Yes, Jazmyn we're done. You can go get changed", Joseph said with a smile and an impressed shake of his head.

After Joseph allowed me to go get changed, I used my

fingers to try to pull the bikini bottoms to cover more of my butt as I stormed away.

As I was changing, I wondered if I'd just ruined any chance of getting a real record-deal, but I felt some solace knowing that I'd done the right thing.

When I came back out, it was now time for them to actually hear me sing. As I went to the stage, I was given a pair of headphones and some music sheets of different songs.

Because I didn't have a demo already done, they were going to record me so they could play it back later.

My singing was going to be divided into 2-parts. One was called the Studio-Performance, where I'd be singing into the mic for recording purposes only. And the other was my Stage-Performance, where they had musicians playing the music and I had to actually give a show for the room of 12-people like it was a stadium full of 12,000.

The sound guy had me speaking into the microphone to test the system.

"Okay, Jazmyn, you've got to get closer to the mic in order for me to get proper levels", the sound guy informed me.

I'd never sung into a stationary microphone before, or one that had a black, circular, netted wind screen. I'd only seen them on television, so I wasn't sure if I was too close.

After the sound guy was satisfied with the levels, it took a couple of tries for me to get started.

The music was playing in the head phones loudly and made it difficult for me because I couldn't hear myself singing or how loud I was singing.

We tried a couple of different things, before the sound

guy aided me by suggesting that I remove the headphones from one ear, so that I could hear the music playing in one ear and myself singing with the other.

I didn't understand why they couldn't just play the music over a stereo and I just sing along until the sound guy explained how it works in recording.

Recording is done on separate tracks, so that things can be changed later. That's how remix's are done using the same vocals from the non-remix version. My voice would be on one track by itself, so that when they listened to it later, they could hear and evaluate only my voice, as though I'd sung the whole song, acappella.

The artists' songs they'd given me to sing varied from up-tempo to ballads to neo-soul. Among the 12-different songs were Janet Jackson's "All For You", Whitney Houston's "I Will Always Love You", Erykah Badu's "On and On" to name just a few.

Honestly, I'd grade my Studio-Performance as a B- to a B, mainly because my focus was distracted from not being able to move around as much while I was singing into the wind screen and still being a little upset with Emily.

As far as my live Stage-Performance, I'd give it an A-, at minimum a B+. Additional time had passed and I enjoyed singing with the band playing behind me much more.

Several times, I had the room jammin' with me as I pulled the wireless mic out of its stand and left the stage to make my way around the conference table as I sang. Even spun the chairs around of a male-executive or two and playfully sat in their laps as I continued belting out verses to show them my alluring side.

The funniest part for me was watching some of these

powerful music executives having trouble keeping the beat as they clapped and rocked side-to-side in a very-white fashion.

After an extremely long and exhausting day, it was near 8:30 PM when Joseph was walking me down the corridor to lead me back to the limo.

"Joseph, thank you for everything", I said genuinely as I prepared to exit.

"No, thank you. You were very good.", he returned.

"I know I didn't sing as well as I know I could've, but that Emily just pissed me off"

"I know, I know. Don't worry about it. I think everyone knows what you're capable of. In any event, you know that I'll stand-up for you!", Joseph promised.

"Well, I appreciate it. And, I'm sorry that I had to speak-up for myself, I didn't mean to make you look bad!"

"Don't worry about that. Actually, I'm proud of you for doing it! Well, it's all up to the staff-meeting now, so I'll be in touch!"

"Okay.", I said, feeling it was the end of our conversation.

Joseph peaked down the corridor before stepping very close to me.

"I'd like to come by your suite later tonight, I just have to wrap-up a few things here, first", he suggested a booty-call, whispering in my ear with both hands on my hips.

Still feeling good for standing-up in the conference room, I wasn't going to fold in the corridor.

"I'on't know. I'm kinda tired, Joseph. I'll call you

when I get back to Atlanta", I said, making it clear that I was nobody's concubine.

"Alright, you do that! Call me.", he semi backed-off, but still assertive enough to place a kiss on my lips.

I pulled my head back from his kiss enough to gain respect, but not so much as to make him hate me.

As I turned to finish my walk down the corridor to the limo, I paused briefly as my eyes were met by Curtis', who'd seen the kiss through the glass doors.

I dug Curtis, so I didn't want him thinking the wrong thing.

Apparently he already was as he greeted me in a business-style, more than what'd be necessary to fool Joseph who was waving good-bye.

We didn't talk at all for the first 3-minutes in the car.

"Curtis, I don't want you to think that I'm......", I tried to explain.

"Look, it's none of my business. It's cool, I'm just the driver", he said coldly.

"Well, do you mind if I climb up in the front?", I asked, leaning forward over the seat.

"I'd prefer it if you didn't. But like I said, I'm just the driver. You're free to do whatever you want!"

I slumped back into the backseat and stared in frustration out of the side window.

I think Curtis thought that I was one of those phony women that acted like status didn't matter to them, yet it really did.

But what made it worse was that it wasn't my fault. Joseph kissed me. Curtis must've seen that I'd pulled my head back from Joseph, therefore he should've known that it meant that I wasn't down with that.

Despite my best efforts to try to change the mood with Curtis, I was destined to spend my last night alone in New York.

I could've called him to make him take me somewhere, so that I'd have a chance to get him to respond to me as he had before. But doing that would make it worse, I thought, so I left it alone.

Seeing as I was without company, I spent half-the-night trying to reach Brea on the phone with no luck, which really frustrated me because I had a lot I wanted to talk about. The audition, confirmation of my pick-up time from the airport tomorrow and the situation with Curtis, which I thought she might have some helpful suggestions before it got too late in the evening.

I figured Brea's ass was out somewhere kickin' it and either didn't have her cell phone with her or had turned it off, so not to get a call from a different man than the one she was probably out with.

Chapter Eleven

On Sunday, when I arrived back in Atlanta on the last flight at 9:00 PM, Brea wasn't on-time to pick me up. I waited for over an hour, as I called her cell phone number and our home telephone number over and over again.

Pissed, doesn't even begin to describe what I felt. And, I couldn't believe that she'd forget to pick me up after I had let her borrow my car for the whole weekend. She was probably out somewhere kickin' it with one of the thug-men she tended to like.

I didn't wanna call my dad for a ride and hear his comments, nor did I feel like catching the Marta-train with my luggage, especially so late at night. To take a taxi would cost over $50, so I called Simeon instead.

It took Simeon about an hour to get to the airport

from his condo. I asked him if he'd seen Brea at all this weekend, he'd not. He called Jamal to ask had he been with her and he said no too.

Normally, I'd be worried if that were the case with Trina, but with Brea, I was almost certain that she was just being inconsiderate.

As we pulled up to my apartment building at 11:40 PM, I didn't see my car anywhere in the parking lot.

Simeon helped me carry my bags into my apartment and offered to stay, but I declined. I'd already asked enough of him by getting him out of bed and spending 2-hours picking me up, dropping me off and driving back to his condo. Plus, I was mad as hell and didn't want him seeing me in the state I'd be in when Brea finally showed up.

I grabbed a pillow and a blanket from my bedroom, not even bothering to put my luggage away and lied on the sofa so that I'd wake-up whenever Brea came through the door.

It was almost 2 o'clock in the morning when I heard keys rattling outside the front door of the apartment.

I sat up and wiped the sleep from my eyes so that I'd look like I'd been awake all night and waited for Brea to open the door.

Her face looked shocked to see that I was awake and waiting for her. She uncharacteristically looked like crap. Her clothes were wrinkly and her hair was messed-up.

"Where in the hell have you been?!", I started right in on her.

"Jaz, I'm in no mood for it right now!", she said shaking her head and walking towards her room like she wasn't going to give me the courtesy of an argument she'd well-deserved.

"Hold up, bitch! How you goin' fuckin' walk away from me after driving my car all fuckin' weekend and leaving me stranded at the fuckin' airport?!", I yelled at her.

"Who you fuckin' callin' a bitch?!", Brea said turning around and pointing her finger like she was preparing to fight me.

I didn't give a damn. If it had to be on, then it was just gonna be on. So, I stood-up and walked around the sofa with my arms extended outward telling her to come on, if that's what she wanted to do. I wasn't scared of her.

"You the only one acting like a bitch! What's up?!", I said with intensity in my eyes.

Brea was surprised by my demeanor and reduced her volatile hand-gestures after I showed her that I was ready for a fight.

"Jaz, I got arrested on Saturday night!", she blurted out.

I paused for a moment.

"Arrested?! For what?", I asked.

"Bootlegging CDs at the club"

It explained why she wasn't at the airport on time. But, it didn't reduce my anger at her.

"Where's my car?", I asked.

"At the Impound", she hated to admit.

"Why is MY car at the Impound?!", I moved a step closer to her.

"I parked it in the lot by the club on Saturday, but after I got arrested, it was still in the lot. I didn't get released until I got someone to pay the bail today. We just went by the parking lot and the car had been towed because the parking fee wasn't paid for today", she tried to explain.

"Mmmmph. Mmmmmph", I breathed anger while shaking my head. "TO-MOR-ROW! We're going to get my car! And you're gonna pay for it!"

"Jaz, I don't have any money! The fine is $175", Brea felt that she'd better declare.

"What the fuck?!", I screamed. "So I'm s'ppose to pay $175 to get MY car that's in the Impound because of YOU? Naw, naw, you better get one of them niggas you be fuckin' to give you some money!"

"Jaz, the police took all my money as evidence. But, I'ma get your money! It might not be tomorrow, but I'll get it!"

"Uhn-uhn! I'ma get my car out tomorrow! That's for sure!", I definitively informed her, as a more pressing issue came to mind. "You fuckin' up Brea! What about fuckin' rent that we gotta pay in 7-days? How you gonna get $175 for the car AND $450 for the rent??"

"I'ma get it! I told you I would, so I'ma have it!", she said, having the nerve to get a little louder.

"You betta! Do me a favor, don't say shit else to me! Just have my money!", I ended our argument by snatching my pillow and bed-cover from sofa and walking to my room.

I'm not a violent person, but beating the shit out of her right then would've felt good. At the same time, I couldn't remove myself from blame because I knew who Brea was and I had no business loaning her my car in the first place.

I wondered which one of her many men had bailed her out of jail? I knew that it wasn't Jamal 'cause he hadn't seen her, but my rage killed my ability to be nosey and I sure wasn't gonna help her by changing the subject, which was money for my car and her half of the rent.

I don't know how she did it, but I didn't really give a damn.

Four days later, Brea not only had the rent money, but also paid me back the $175 for the Impound-fine, plus an extra $100 as apology-money.

The extra $100-bill didn't fix it for me, but shit, I took it.

I figured she'd gotten money from Demetrius, one of her hoodlicious drug-dealing men.

It always tripped me out how Brea could date someone like Demetrius and at the same time be mad at her brother who had gone to jail doing the same thing.

I called Demetrius hoodlicious because he didn't look hard like a drug-dealer, he was actually sexy, cute and somewhat intelligent. Had a look kinda like rapper MA$E. Although he acted thuggish, it was clear that he'd be one to say *'yes mam'* when his mama was around.

Though I never confirmed it, I figured it must've been him that helped her out.

At the beginning of December, money was tight for me. My job as a trainer wasn't working out because business had slowed-down, people were saving their money to buy Christmas gifts and not spending money on personal training sessions.

I didn't know how I was gonna make money for next month's bills.

Joseph Myers had called me in November to let me know that the record-label wasn't going forward with me as a solo artist, but would consider me as a member of a group that they may be forming. The problem was that he didn't know when it would be. It could be as much as 8-months to a year-and-a-half.

I'd receive no additional money from them until details were actually worked out and I'd have to audition all over again, which I knew I wasn't down for, so I passed.

Brea suggested that I come to work with her. She'd gotten a couple gigs, I wouldn't really call them jobs, but at least she was out of the bootleg business.

One of the places Brea worked a couple of nights a week was at *Slick-N-Thick*, a local strip-club. She'd started back in October, when she needed to earn quick money to pay me back and pay the rent.

For Brea, it was conflicting feelings she got from working there. She was an attention-hog, so she loved the feeling guys gave her in the club, but I think she also felt like she was too good to be just a stripper and that's why she only did it a couple of times a week. Unless of course, she saw some nice outfits that she wanted to buy. Then her greed would make her dance a day or two more.

I wasn't really down for the stripper-thang, not even

once, as I had my career to think about, not to mention my parents lived Atlanta.

Where Brea worked most often was a place called *Reflex*, an upscale massage therapy salon on Pleasant Hill Road in the city of Duluth, Georgia.

I figured that I could make pretty good money there once I'd built a customer base because the rates were high, about $150 per hour and the massage therapist got to keep 50% of that.

I didn't know how to give a massage, but *Reflex* was willing to train without me having to pay to go to massage school. That's what Brea had done.

So that's what I'd planned to do, work at *Reflex* as I tried to get my music career off the ground.

I figured that I'm in Hotlanta, as much talent as there is here, it should be easy enough to find gigs or form my own group and get signed by SoSoDef or LaFace Records.

Plus, I knew it was very possible that Brea would sooner or later end-up hookin' up with someone in the music biz that had connections and I'd be put on too.

About a week before Christmas, I was still working at the gym because *Reflex* didn't have a job opening until February.

It was at the gym where I got a surprise telephone call.

"Hello"

"Hi, Jazmyn", the voice sounded familiar even through the sniffling.

"Trina??", I questioned.

"Yes"

"It's so good to hear your voice! What's wrong?", I asked concerned.

"It's...nothin'... I just...awh...nothing", Trina debated disclosing.

"Gurll, it's okay. Where are you? I'ma come meet you right now!", I spoke with assurance.

I told my boss that I had an emergency and left the gym on my way to meet Trina who'd parked her car and was aimlessly walking around downtown Atlanta near the Underground Mall.

Her parents had the worst fight ever. Divorce was now a certainty, as Mr. Whitfield had moved-out of the house they'd just purchased and into a luxury apartment complex near his new dealership.

I'm sure she hated to call me, but she knew deep-down that I was a true friend, even despite the mistake that I'd made concerning Brea and Jamal.

I found Trina sitting silently on a bench in the Underground Mall's outdoor courtyard area. She was shivering because it was cold, but apparently wanted to be alone as she'd chosen to stay outside over the warmth of the inside of the mall.

"Tree-nah?", I called her name as I got close to her.

Trina turned around slowly and I could see the white streaks of dried tears vividly on her dark complexion face.

"Hey Jaz", Trina meekly responded, as I sat down next to her rather than suggesting moving to a warmer location.

"I'on't know what to do?", she began speaking, not knowing where to begin.

"I know. I know.", I said with compassion and risking putting an arm around her. "I know this is hard to hear, but there's really nothing for you to do. This situation isn't about you. It's about them. Just know that they BOTH love you"

The tears resumed for Trina and I was battling my own tears with all my might, so that I'd appear strong for her.

I knew that her parents meant the world to her. And their union represented promise of what was possible. With that now gone, she was confused, about everything.

We sat huddled together for 20-minutes in the cold. I didn't care how it might appear to by-passers. I was consoling my girl in her hour of need, so I didn't give a damn what people I didn't even know might've been thinking about.

I'd heard my own parents yelling at each other many times and even talking about divorce, but they always worked it out. So, it was tough to imagine what emotions must be running through Trina's body.

When Trina gradually ascended from her distraught state, I wanted to apologize for the Brea-Jamal situation, but it didn't seem appropriate because it paled by comparison to her parents' divorce. Still, I didn't want her to think that I was just not trying to accept responsibility.

"Trina, I know this is off the subject, but I just wanted to say that I'm sorry. You know, about the Brea-Jamal thing", I offered with sincere eyes.

"I know. It's no big deal. Don't worry about it", she

said genuinely.

"Yeah, it is a big deal. I'm your friend and that wasn't acting like it and I'm really, really, really sorry", I continued, making sure that I apologized enough, just in case her acceptance of it was due solely to her dealing with a larger issue at the time of my apology.

"I know. I really didn't care about that as much as that you guys were hiding it from me. That's what really hurt me, but I'm over it now.", she explained quickly before changing the subject to not make me wallow in guilt, "I'm cold!"

"Woo! Me too! I thought you'd never get cold and I was gonna stay here as long as you wanted. C'mon, let's go to my apartment", I suggested, knowing that she'd appreciate a break from going home where all the stress was.

We got in my car and I drove Trina to her car, so that she could follow me to my apartment. On the way, I called Brea to update her on the situation, so she'd not fuck it up. Also, made sure that she was gonna apologize to Trina as soon as we walked through the door. Thankfully, she did.

Chapter Twelve

In late January, Brea had to cover most of the bills for the month because I just didn't have it.

I planned to start paying her back once I got my job at *Reflex*.

Trina was struggling too, as her parents' divorce was getting extremely ugly. Accounts had been frozen to prevent either party from unfairly using money until a final court-decision had been made, which reduced the normal free-flowing money she normally got from her parents.

Mr. and Mrs. Whitfield were strapped for cash paying each of their attorney's fees, mortgage on the house, Mr. Whitfield's apartment rent, Trina's tuition, among other bills.

At my suggestion, Trina moved-in temporarily with

us at the beginning of January to stay out of the fray of the divorce.

When I informed Brea, she thought that Trina should pay a third of the rent.

After I threatened to smack the taste out of her mouth if she even so much as mentioned it to Trina, the friend we'd already betrayed once, Brea let it go.

Brea was making good money at both places, *Reflex* and *Slick-N-Thick*.

My music career wasn't going as smooth as I'd thought it would go. The best gig I'd been able to get was singing Christmas songs during the holidays at a few local malls for little cash.

When I needed to rely on Brea to pay some of the bills, she suggested that I at least check-out *Slick-N-Thick* as a possible source of income. She wasn't pressuring me because I owed her money, so I did go by the club.

Trina and I went by on one of the days Brea was working to survey the scene. I watched dollar bills flowing like water.

I was surprised to find that it was nothing like I imagined.

Originally, I thought I'd feel awkward as a woman in a strip club, but there were many women there. Some were obviously gay, but most were not. It was more of a hang-out place. Like a sports-bar that happen to have nude dancing.

There were pool tables and a vast array of televisions tuned to sports games.

Though the atmosphere was a pleasant surprise and I was desperate, I just couldn't bring myself to do it.

Me and Trina laughed as the DJ called Brea to the stage by her stage-name, "Next booty on duty, Cool Breeze".

Brea smiled as we watched her during her routine that included acrobatic pole maneuvers.

"It's not that bad working in here", Trina commented to me.

"Gurrll, you trippin'!", I said with a surprise look.

"Naw, I'm just saying, it ain't that bad", Trina returned bobbing her head to the beat of the music as she watched Brea accepting bill after bill in her g-string from guys that kept coming up to her on the stage.

The more money Brea received, the more clothing she removed until she was completely naked.

"What are you sayin'? You'd actually consider working here?", I asked an entranced Trina.

"Mmmmm. Maybe. It's just nudity.", she said undeterred.

Trina's outlook on life had changed dramatically after her parents' split. Three-months ago, she'da been offended at the mere suggestion of her being a stripper. It was like she was a whole different person.

The increase in confidence was good, but I think she was over-compensating for her years of inhibition, too much too fast.

When Trina vacated her seat to go place a bill in Brea's g-string, I wanted to hide my face from embarrassment, but the room seemed unaffected by it. No one was staring at the sight of a woman tipping a woman.

After Brea got off stage, she came by us at the bar.

"Brea, you are truly wild!", I said to Brea, referring to

161

her upside-down, sliding down the pole with her legs open in a V-position.

"Shhh, gurrll! Don't be using my real name in here", Brea spoke.

"Can I buy you a drink?", one man came up to Brea and offered.

"Jimmy, I'll take an *'Incredible Hulk'*", Brea answered to the bartender and not to the guy who'd offered, like it was a done-deal at the moment he offered.

The *Incredible Hulk* was a very popular and potent drink in the ATL. A mix of Hypnotic and Hennessey, when meshed together, it turned green in color, hence its name.

"When you get the drink, I'm over there", the man said pointing to his table, after happily paying for the drink, "I wanna get a couple of dances from you"

"I'll be over in a minute. Hey, these are my girls. They're thirsty too", Brea made sure to say before he left.

The man gave her a $20-bill to pay for our drinks and went back to his table to wait for Brea.

"I ain't mad at you, Brea!", Trina said, sounding impressed how she seemed to rule the club.

"Hey, I'ma go dance for him and before you guys leave, I got someone I want y'all to meet", Brea said as she winced while taking a sip from her drink before going to meet the man.

Brea's superior dancing skills combined with her stunning beauty and sassy attitude really suited her for this line of work.

While she was dancing for one guy, I could witness other men at different tables sneaking peeks. Even some of the men peeking were already getting dances and ignored their dancer to view Brea.

Brea was one of the best-looking women in the club, and that was saying a lot, as there were many gorgeous women dancing.

It was strange learning more about my friend's body than I ever thought I'd ever know. Seeing moles in places I never would've seen in ten years of being roommates. I'd already seen her little-girl nipples before, but I never knew that she had one of those over-sized clits until today. And the fellas loved staring at it, as she'd eagerly show it to them.

We watched Brea grind on the man that paid for our drinks for 10-consecutive songs. He couldn't get enough of her.

At $10 per song, I watched Brea make $100 in a little over a half-hour while I sat there dead-broke, sipping a free drink that had been brokered by Brea.

Once she began getting dressed again, Brea held-up one finger to let us know that she'd be right back.

She then disappeared behind a wall that I assumed led to the dressing room and returned about 15-minutes later cloaked in a new sexy black bikini-like outfit with a shear see-through top.

"That's kee-ute, girl!", I couldn't help but compliment.

"Oh, thanks! I just bought it from the house-mom in the dressing room. I was gonna introduce you to someone, but I don't see him right now. I'm tellin' you guys, you oughtta think about working here. Easiest money you'll ever make!", Brea suggested.

"I-C!", Trina returned enthusiastically.

163

"Oh, Trina, they'd love YOU here! The fellas love asses up in here. You'd make a fortune!", Brea proposed to Trina.

I didn't like her dangling the carrot in front of Trina while she was in a vulnerable state.

"Trina, you've got school. When would you have time?", I tried to interject doubt.

"Jaz, you see her over there", Brea said pointing to another girl dancing, "She's Pre-Med at Georgia State. Trina, you could come by on amateur night. Check it out!"

Having had my raising-of-doubt easily conquered, I relinquished even trying anymore.

"I might just do that", Trina was beginning to be won-over, as I shook my head.

"Herman! Herman!", Brea yelled over the loud club music to a well-dressed man, while waving him over.

"Hey, wassup, Cool Breeze", the man addressed Brea with a hug and a peck on her cheek.

Herman was a very handsome guy, but noticing the wedding-ring on his finger, I wondered why he'd given Brea a kiss on the cheek.

"Herman, these are my friends, Jazmyn and Trina", she introduced.

"Nice to meet both of you", he said with a contagious smile.

"Herman and his wife own this club and the Caramel Club", Brea explained proudly. "Is your wife here?"

"She's in the back doing some business", Herman replied, as someone else was now calling his name.

"Trina was thinking about dancing", Brea blurted out.

"Oh, really? Well, stand-up, let me look at you", Herman said playfully and somehow managed to do it without sounding pretentious.

Trina blushed as she stood up and Brea pushed her to spinning around.

"Damn, girl! Now where'd you get a body like that!", Herman said impressed by Trina's butt.

"She got it from her mama!", Brea made a joke by singing the lyrics of the song by the same name.

"Look, anytime you're ready, come see me! Brea can let you know the deal. It was nice to meet you both!", Herman charmingly said as he left towards the person who'd called his name several times.

Herman was clearly 'Da Man'. I could tell by the diamond encrusted watch and the pristine clothes that he was wearing. But mostly, because everyone greeted him like a king.

"He was nice. I never would've guessed that he'd be the owner", I said to Brea after he'd left.

"He and his wife, Tyanna are real cool peeps", Brea informed.

"I wonder how they got so much money to own two clubs?", Trina expressed my sentiments exactly.

Herman looked to be no older than 30.

Brea giggled like she had inside information.

"What's so funny?", I inquired.

"Herman used to be a porn-star!", Brea disclosed her secret and intensely watched for our reaction.

"Whaaaattt?", Trina and I said in unison as we lowered our eyes to Herman's crotch-level while he was

165

conversing with another dancer, like we were gonna be able to see some evidence.

"Uhn-hun, I see y'all lookin'!! He's got it, I hear. His name in the movies was 'King-Kong'. I'm not kidding, 14-INCHES!!", Brea nodded to us. "I ain't seen it. But that's what some of the other girls said and I believe 'em."

"14-INCHES?! Damn, I wouldn't wanna be his wife!", I exclaimed.

"C'mon??? You wouldn't be curious enough to wanna try it once?", Trina surprised me by questioning both of us, especially because I knew she couldn't handle Jamal's twelve.

"HELL, NAW!! 14-INCHES should qualify as Assault with a Deadly Weapon!", I laughed my answer.

"I'on't know? Maybe once, but I couldn't have that shit up in me every night!", Brea answered with surprising common-sense. "I've been meaning to rent one of his videos to check him out!", Brea added with all seriousness.

I secretly hoped that she would get the video, 'cause there was something intriguing about seeing someone that you've actually met in a porn movie. But honestly, it was mostly about the 14-Inch thang.

My curiosity also peaked regarding seeing his wife. I was interested to see the woman that was able to routinely take 14-Inches.

I never did get the chance to see Herman's wife, as she never came out from the back and we left about an hour later.

Chapter Thirteen

I was happy when February finally rolled-around, yet nervous. You'd think I was going to a big music label audition rather than orientation at *Reflex*.

I'd already quit my job at the gym, even though business was beginning to pick-up again.

I loved my job at the gym and the people, but I was just ready for a change.

Also, it was calming to know that I was going to be able to earn more money to pay Brea back, though she never made an issue of it. But still, I just didn't like owing someone.

Trina had danced for one weekend at *Slick-N-Thick*, but decided that it wasn't for her and I was glad that she did. Even more so, that she'd come to that conclusion on her own.

She was still living with us and planned to earn some money working part-time at *Reflex* as well.

Orientation was on a Tuesday morning at 10:00 AM before they officially opened at Noon.

Brea went with us, even though she wasn't scheduled to work on that day.

"Hey, Hung! Hey, Sumy", Brea greeted the late-20's husband-n-wife Asian owners.

"What's poppin', Brea?", Hung, the husband greeted Brea in an unexpected hip-hop style, without as much as a hint of an Asian-accent.

They both looked like they could've been mixed with some other race, though I couldn't tell what race.

He was taller than most men of Asian-descent I'd seen, about 5'10 or so and one of his hobbies clearly must've been working-out. His chest and arms were well developed and visible through the form-fitting, thin, V-neck sweater he had on over a plain black t-shirt.

Hung's wife Sumy, pronounced *Soo-Me*, was short and small in stature, about 5'2. She was truly beauty-pageant cute, armed with a well balanced-shape of petite curves, a glowing smile with dimpled cheeks and silky-ish black hair that'd been curled into a style.

Unlike Hung, Sumy did posses a tinge of an Asian-accent, as though she might not have been born in the United States and English was her second-language. But what made it more noticeable was her speech could be a little choppy as she often omitted key verbs or adverbs as she spoke.

To the eye, Hung and Sumy made for a very pretty

couple.

Her personality was out-going too, but less than Hung who already appeared to be a bit of a hip-hop party-animal, which was surprising and not just because of his race. Sumy wasn't your stereo-typical quiet Asian female either.

It was just that judging by the elegant design of *Reflex*, which had been nicely renovated from a bank to a massage salon with its Mahogany-wood counters, over-sized aquariums filled with exotic fish, white Roman-pedestal pillars, and even its location seemed to cater more to a stoic upscale white crowd. So, it made it odd to picture that Hung and Sumy would be the owners. But, I could also tell that they were serious about business and would give their breed of customer exactly the image that they wanted.

"These are my girls I was tellin' you about. This is Jazmyn and Trina", Brea introduced both of us.

"Welcome to Reflex, ladies. My name is Hung and this is my wife, Sumy", Hung charmed by stepping forward and gently shaking both of our hands, followed by his wife doing the same.

"Soo-mee, that's a pretty name. Does it mean something?", Trina inquired.

"Thank you. Yes. Sumy mean flower"

"That's cool. I wish my name meant something", I commented.

"Do you want to know what my name means?", Hung said clowning around with a smile, that made Brea laugh immediately and Sumy roll her eyes at him.

It took a moment for me and Trina to get the joke as we had to recall his name first before laughing ourselves.

"I think we have an idea", I flirted back.

We spent a few minutes filling out forms in the lobby before Sumy guided us to the back, passed several tanning tables, a vault that hadn't been removed since its transformation from a bank, and into one of the 14-massage rooms for training.

When we entered the room, Hung was already lying on the table underneath a white sheet, apparently going to be our guinea-pig, as Sumy began training us in the art of massage.

"First ask customer if like music. Always begin customer on back", Sumy explained.

I had to really concentrate on what she was saying because of her inferior English.

"Now, Brea show what do next", Sumy spoke as she directed Brea to begin massaging Hung while she explained techniques.

Brea used warms oils on Hung's muscular back as her hands firmly glided up and down.

We were taught techniques on how to move the arm, so that we could reach muscles behind the shoulder blade, the correct way to loosen tightened calf, hamstring and glute muscles.

Watching Brea's ability made me jealous of the relaxed Hung, 'cause I wanted a massage. Now I understood why people were willing to pay so much for this service.

After learning all of the techniques of the back and even participating, Hung was turned to lying on his back.

Brea supported his head in her hands by holding onto the back of his neck, as she guided each hand, one at a time on each side of his neck. Then she used her thumbs to press tension away from his upper-peck muscles on his chest.

Soon, I was ignoring completely Sumy's narration of techniques, as it was easier to learn by watching anyway.

"They down with Special?", Hung questioned up to Brea.

"Yeah, they're down", Brea answered on our behalf.

"Okay, now. Brea show Special", Sumy said.

"What's the Special?", I asked.

"You see now. You do Special. Special make you lot of money!", Sumy encouraged.

Brea smiled at us as she made her way to the other end of table and lifted the sheet to reveal a nude Hung.

Immediately I had an idea of how Brea'd been making so much money without dancing at the club that often.

Trina had her hand over her mouth as Brea put on some latex gloves, lubed and gripped Hung's dick in her hands.

"Must use gloves. Always gloves. Keep towel nearby", Sumy said, un-impacted that Brea was holding her husband's dick.

Brea stroked his thang relentlessly until it was standing taller than I expected. It wasn't quite his namesake, though it was a good 7-to-8 inches.

His name should've been Thick instead of Hung, as the circumference of his thang was unbelievable. It was more plump than a Ballpark hotdog, about the width of freshly-bought family-size tube of tooth paste.

"Hand only. Never mouth!", I faintly heard Sumy

continue instructing.

My visual senses were now dominating my hearing as I watched Hung lying just as comfortable as could be with his fingers interlocked behind his head.

"Also, always lock door, first. Very important, door locked", Sumy repeated.

After about 14-minutes of Brea's tugging at Hung's thang and massaging of his balls, I was impressed that he'd not cum yet.

"Talking okay, if customer like. But softly", Sumy said nodding for Brea to give examples by doing so.

"Does that feel good? You like that? Ooo, you're so hard. I like your big dick in my hands. I want you to cum in my hands. Are you gonna cum for me?", Brea ran through the list of suggested comments routinely, as she continued.

"Ummm. Ummm.", Hung began moaning as Brea's hands were finally beginning to get to him.

Me and Trina were trippin' watching Sumy smile at the sounds of her husband's nearing orgasm.

"You gonna cum for me Hung?", Brea now asked more sincerely.

"Uuugh. Uuugh. Uuugh", Hung started chanting more frequently.

Brea's hands stayed one step ahead of Hung's chanting pace until she was moving them in turbo-fast speed and Hung's head lifted from its relaxed position.

"Watch carefully!", Sumy said urgently to get our attention.

Just as Hung began to cum, Brea had placed her hand over the top of his thang to prevent his explosion from going everywhere in the room.

After Hung's body neared completion, Brea used the towel to clean him up a bit, then removed her gloves and placed them in the center of the towel before opening a metal door chute that was installed in the wall and throwing them down it.

"That's incinerator. No evidence. Do right away. Never wait. Do as soon as he's done", Sumy further instructed, referring to what the chute led to.

After the show was over, reality struck me.

I've given up my other job to become a dick-massager?, I thought to myself.

I felt like Brea had misled me all along about what I was getting into.

Trina didn't seem to be in as deep of thought as me, as she was smiling wide enough to almost see all of her molar-teeth.

"Simple, right?", Sumy questioned, I think to see if we were down with that.

"Oh, piece of cake!", Trina quickly returned, as though she wanted to start working that moment.

"Now we show female Special", Sumy said, climbing onto the table as my jaw hit the floor. "Female want Special sometime too".

Hung stood next to us wrapped in a towel and smiling as Brea had put on a new pair of gloves and caressed all over Sumy's petite body.

Sumy had tried to be the massage-ee and instructor until Brea's touch made it impossible, so Hung took over.

My mind couldn't decide on which shock to focus on. The fact that I was watching two women, or that Brea was one of the two, or that I was shocked by sweet little Sumy's behavior.

Trina was folded-over laughing out-loud, as Brea had massaged and pinched Sumy's breasts until her almost-black-girl-dark colored nipples were hard.

Soon, Brea's feverishly moving hand between Sumy's legs had her tiny body jerking, her petite thighs shivering out of control, as her face intensified, her eyes rolled, she gritted her teeth and even broke into moans in her native Asian dialect.

I laughed too, once she was speaking in a foreign language.

Even once Brea had ceased, Sumy's head continued to jerk side-to-side as though she were trying to shake off the orgasm.

"You guys can do this, right?", Hung stared at us.

"Oh, no problem", Trina said enthusiastically.

"Yeah", I conceded.

At least it's discreet and I ain't a stripper, I made an excuse in my head.

It was true, though. I didn't have to dance naked or give up no pussy. So, I wasn't being a hoe.

I'll admit, it was interesting to watch Brea and Sumy, though I really wasn't down with the woman thang, but I figured I'd tell them that later.

Chapter Fourteen

It was mid-March when I got my first break in the music biz.

Of all things, working at *Reflex* had led to meeting Brandon Winwood, a music producer that was a client of mine.

After giving him one of my better hand jobs, he'd informed me that he was looking for a lead singer for one of the groups he was producing that had a sound similar to the Black Eyed Peas band.

Brandon was a Ludacris look-alike, with the afro and everything that he sometimes wore braided.

I was no fool. I could tell that there was something a little strange about his music company, Twisted Records, from my first visit to the Stone Mountain studios.

The receptionist was a gum-popping brickhouse-hoochie that wore shirts so small that they had her clearly augmented-breasts in jeopardy of spilling out at any moment.

Besides that and the ever-present smell of marijuana, some of the management he'd chosen to employ looked like they'd responded to a for-hire ad placed in the Penitentiary-Times newspaper. And on Pay-Day, I watched him pay them all in cash.

It seemed that the studio might've been funded by some drug money because of all the cash that floated around.

But I guess I can't automatically say that with certainty, as Hung sometimes paid me with cash out of enormous stacks of money he had stored in the vault. My guess was Hung and Sumy had at least $150,000 in cash in the vault that they were obviously hiding from the IRS. A lot of clients chose to pay that way for secrecy purposes, not wanting traceable transaction receipts.

All in all, I was still dead-set on taking this opportunity because I'd already learned my lesson about being picky.

I really had no other options and Brandon had the juice in the business. His label was starting to become the talk of the nation, as some of the artists he produced were featured on some major artists' CDs, though none as of yet had a mega-success CD of their own.

My thought was that I could become his first full-fledged break-out star.

Brea had been kicked-off the Atlanta Hawks Cheerleading team for missing rehearsals. But she didn't give a damn because she'd only used it as a way to get to affluent men and for the attention, which she was getting plenty of at the strip-club. And between *Reflex* and *Slick-N-Thick*, spending money wasn't a problem either.

It was Brea's never-ending appetite for the good-life that helped her spend it just as fast as she got it. She even purchased a portable closet for her room to accommodate the amount of clothes she'd bought that overwhelmed her built-in closet.

But what was her most extravagant purchase was a brand new Mercedes convertible she obtained only through some creative financing techniques, made solely possible by one of the men she'd met at the club that worked for a Mercedes dealership.

I always expected that I'd one day see the Repo-man towing her car down the street, once it was discovered that the paperwork had been forged, should she ever miss a single payment.

Her latest hobby, or at least that's what I called it, was another scheme for attention and a way to meet more ballers – auditioning to dance in music videos.

I think she was trying to become the new Melyssa Ford or something. But not quite as serious about the career move as her. It was more about the challenge that fueled Brea.

Brea'd taken some shots with a famous ATL photographer, Charles A. Brown and appeared on several party-fliers, local artists' CD covers, calendars and even some best-selling book-covers.

The shoot was done *TFP*, which is an industry term

that meant *Trade For Portfolio*, so it was unpaid. But the benefit was that she got to keep the incredible-looking professionally-done photos to use in a portfolio to show to talent-managers whenever she was auditioning for videos or modeling gigs.

Both me and Trina got some photos done too, mostly from vanity, although I could actually use mine for business. It was the fact that he was willing to accept us to model for him that was exciting, as his schedule was extremely busy and he was very selective. Not just anyone could model for him, so that made us feel good.

Trina had grown comfortable with her newly-developed, Brea-induced wilder side.

It amazed me how she was able to keep-up with school, work part-time at *Reflex* and still kick-it at wild parties with Brea. Not to mention, she was catching the baller-bug from Brea, as she was starting to also date for income.

I thought that it might just be a temporary thing while her parents weren't able to finance her as they'd done before their accounts had been frozen, but it was unsettling viewing how much she enjoyed playing men for money.

"What's up Jamal?", I said unenthused.

"Nothin'. Is Brea here?", he asked as he made his way into the apartment, not waiting for an invitation.

"No. Brea's not here, Jamal", I said, still standing by the door trying to send the message that I was tired of his unexpected visits.

Brea had several ballers now. Jamal was just one of them and reduced to the bench-squad.

The less attention she gave Jamal, the more he resorted to surprise visits at the apartment and I was getting tired of being Brea's receptionist.

Also bothering me was the fact that Trina had fucked Jamal again as payback to Brea, though Brea didn't know that. It was just a personal thing for Trina to know that she could reclaim a man from Brea if she wanted to.

In either case, I hated being in the middle of this ghetto-drama.

Trina's stupid-ass confided what she'd done to me and also let Jamal know that I knew, which had him feeling like he was *The Man*.

"Trina here?", Jamal questioned looking around.

"Nobody's here but me, Jamal", I sighed frustration, still holding on to the door handle and my hand on my hip. "I'll have which ever one of them you want to call you when they get back"

"Why you always be hatin' on me?", Jamal said as he walked close up on me.

"'Cause you triflin'!", I responded as I pushed him back off of me.

"Why I gotta be triflin'? I'm just satisfying", he said like he was the mack.

"Whatevah. I gotta go Jamal", I said, trying to end our conversation by re-opening the door.

Jamal exited, but not before purposely and seductively brushing his body past mine, making contact with my breasts.

"I'on't know why you be playing? You know you want some! I know that you've heard about it", Jamal leaned over to brag in a whisper.

"BYE JAMAL!", I said, firmly closing the door on him.

It was clear that Jamal's goal was to be able to claim that he'd fucked everyone in our household. But that wasn't gonna ever be true, unless I moved out.

Me and Simeon had a thing going-on, not super-serious, but still a thing nevertheless.

Despite my best attempts to convince otherwise, Jamal knew I'd never share his attempts at me with his boy, Simeon. First, because I'd already bluffed to do so and hadn't. And second, because I had previously proven twice before that I wouldn't when he was sneaking with Brea on Trina, and now with Trina on Brea.

I ain't gonna lie, Jamal was fine, had a gorgeous body, and of course I knew that he really knew how to fuck.

If it weren't for the reason as to why he was tryin' to mack on me, I might've. But, that was the point. So I wasn't tryin' to prove him right about me and I didn't care what Brea and Trina were willing to do or were already doing. That was their business.

The best way for me to keep my curiosity from getting the better of me and impacting my judgment was to limit solo time with him, which is what I did.

After Jamal left, I went to the studio to lay down some hook-tracks for another artists' album. I didn't mind doing that, especially the first time I heard my voice on the radio. But I was impatient and ready to get the group Brandon had brought me in for, started.

Brandon always claimed to be waiting for the right moment to release us. Plus he wanted to get my voice to a recognizable level to help with sales when our CD dropped.

That sounded good, but the truth was that he'd done little more than introduce me to the other group members and selected a name for the band, Chocolate Cream.

All of my time spent at the studio was laying down hooks, background vocals and getting coffee. We'd not even recorded one song for Chocolate Cream.

For the music industry's claim that things moved fast, all I ever knew about was waiting. I was ready to hold a mic in my hands instead of dicks at *Reflex*.

When I came in from another frustrating late night at the studio, Brea was waiting to talk to me.

"W'sup, Jaz?", Brea said.

"Same old shit at the studio", I returned.

"Don't worry about it girl, you'll get your chance!", she encouraged.

I appreciated the words, but it didn't change my mood as I went into the kitchen to warm-up some left-over Chinese food in the microwave.

It was late and I just noticed that Trina was not asleep on the pull-out sofa bed.

"Where's Trina?", I asked.

"She went out with Kwame", Brea informed.

Kwame was one of the ballers she'd met a few weeks back at a White-Linen party at Excursion nightclub in College Park.

"Jaz, I was thinking about getting my own place", Brea informed.

181

Our lease wasn't up until the end of August, so I was trippin'. Actually, the lease was in my name only because she wasn't in Atlanta when I rented it. But, we both knew that it was our apartment.

"Our lease ain't up until August", I responded confused as to how she was gonna plan to skip on me.

"I know. I know. I wouldn't move-out 'til May. It's just gettin' crowded around here. I'm not tryin' to leave you hangin'. I just figured that now that you and Trina are making money at Reflex, that you guys could handle rent. Plus, school will be out for Trina in May and she'll be able to work more hours. And, you don't have to worry about paying me back any of the money from your half of rent that I already paid", Brea explained considerately.

I didn't really like it. But she had paid the rent during bad times. And my new job was due to her connections. Plus, Trina's temporary residency had turned into a permanent situation.

I guess I could feel her a bit. She was making more loot and I couldn't blame her for wanting more space and comfort.

"Okay, cool, Brea. Let me talk to Trina to make sure that she's gonna stay permanently", I said with just that one condition. "Damn girl. I'm gonna miss you"

"It ain't like we ain't gonna see each other. Hell, we all work at Reflex. And you know we still gonna kick it together", Brea spoke tough, but I could tell that she felt a little somethin' too.

"Well, I know one thing's for sure, we're gonna have to change our damn phone number when you leave, all the niggas you have callin' here", I smiled to rescue the moment from sadness.

"All the calls ain't just for me", she tried to defend.

"Most of them! And now you got Trina damn near getting as many calls as you!", I charged.

"That ain't my fault! Trina's a big girl. She's just doing her thang!", Brea smiled, 'cause she knew damn well how much she'd impacted Trina.

The next day while Trina was in class at Spellman, I was convinced by Brea to go with her to one of her video shoot auditions in Buckhead.

It looked like Hoochie-ville, with all of the damn-near naked women trying to draw the attention of the casting director's eye. And it reminded me of the reason for my hesitancy to come in the first place.

Brea thought it might be a good idea to mingle with other people in the music biz besides Brandon, as a way to make him appreciate more what he had in me.

You could feel the jealousy in the room and smell the potential for a cat-fight at any moment as there were constant smirks and glares between different dancers.

Like most of the video-shoots Brea went to, she had an inside connection, albeit far removed.

A perfect example was today's shoot. Her name had been placed on the Automatic List, which meant that she'd not have to participate in the cattle-call audition process and would automatically be allowed on the set and in the video.

Her contact was an Atlanta club DJ that had a friend who was a radio DJ in St. Louis. The St. Louis radio DJ's childhood friend was the cousin of the band's manager who'd hired the video director.

All of Brea's contacts were so twisted and interconnected that you'd damn near needed a Hook-up version of *Mapquest* to figure them out. But whatever the case, she always made the connection work for her.

I was uncomfortable with the whole scene and didn't see the rush Brea apparently got from this environment. Plus it made me a little more frustrated with my current situation in the music biz. I had no desire to be just another booty in a music video, unless it was my own music video, featuring my own music.

Brea's Automatic List Pass only guaranteed that she'd be in the video, but she'd have to work and tease the mind, really the loin, of the director into making her the star.

"I knew that bitch was gonna be here", Brea said with a twisted face.

"Brea, chill. Who are you talkin' about?", I tried to relax her tone.

"That bitch right there. You remember I told you about a girl named Tonika?"

"Umm-hmm"

"Well, there she is right there. I guarantee, she won't be stealing the show today", Brea said, setting her duffle bags down like she was preparing for a fist-fight.

I vaguely remembered Brea mentioning a dancer that stole the show from her in one the rap videos she'd appeared in. Tonika had been featured in the video over Brea, which pissed her off because she wasn't used to losing. Brea was always spouting about someone, so I paid it no never-mind at the time.

Tonika was very pretty. Every bit as fine as Brea.

Quite possibly, more cute, depending on a guy's taste. Plus, she had a bit of an exotic Somalian-look. Tall and curvaceously thick like a golden-brown colored Serena Williams.

From a distance, I couldn't tell if she was a bitch as Brea described or if it was just Brea's envy.

I had no idea of what Brea planned to do, so I grabbed her by the arm, just in case.

"Hold on, Brea", I whispered sternly.

"Jaz, what's wrong with you?", she questioned just as sternly, looking down at my grip on her arm.

"Brea. You just can't go over and beat her up", I warned.

"Jaz, ain't nobody said anything about fightin'. I ain't gotta beat that bitch's ass to win", Brea explained.

I wasn't sure if she meant that or not. I thought maybe she was just saying it to get me to release my grip of her arm. Cautiously, I did.

"Then what you talkin' about, Brea?", I inquired, knowing that she had a devious plan.

"Oh, I got it covered. Don't worry", Brea said shaking her head.

I was nervous because I knew that Brea had the potential to do just about anything. Strangely, I hoped her plan was just as benign as just giving the director head in the office.

Brea was naturally beautiful, but put little effort into her modeling, unlike some of the women that were auditioning. Stomach muscles were on display all over the place from underneath their cut-off tops and arms were tight and toned.

Brea was fit too, but more of a soft-look fit. In a room of average women, she'd easily stand-out. But in a room full of women that put in hours of work at the gym, even Brea's natural and facial beauty had the ability to be conquered, though it would still take a lot to do it.

Apparently, Tonika had proven it and Brea didn't like it. Instead of resolving to out-work the competition, Brea would resort to tricks. Always taking the easy way out.

I made my way to the office to network by introducing myself as one of Twisted Record's artist, for credibility's-sake. Otherwise, he'da shunned me as just another dancer-wanna-be-singer.

"Oh, hey, nice to meet you, Jazmyn. How's Brandon doing?", the director, Derrick 'Flava' Jones asked.

I was surprised that the mere mention of being a part of Twisted Records gained me so much instant respect with such a world-renown video director, as D-Flava spoke to me like we were old friends.

"He's good", I responded, not really caring to talk about him, instead of me.

"The next time you see B-Wood, tell him to call me. I've got this movie thing coming up that I'm going to need his help on the soundtrack", D-Flava turned me into Brandon's secretary.

I didn't mind though. I was getting behind-the-scenes info about an upcoming movie soundtrack.

"I will", I simply said, before having an incredible idea. "I-igh-igh Will. I-igh-igh-igh-igh Sho-oooh Will", I sang my answer to make myself unforgettable and to show him my vocal ability and range.

D-Flava momentarily paused, as he was intensely listening to my fluttering up the octave scale .

"Damn, girl! You can sang! I KNOW you've got to be B-Wood's next project!", D-Flava complimented. "Wait a minute. I've heard your voice before. You sang the hook on that song, 'Krunk da Funk', didn't you?"

I was impressed that he'd recognized my work, even if it was more of a background role in a marginally successful song.

"Yep, that's me", I said proudly.

"I see Twisted's got it going on over there with the new talent!", D-Flava expressed excited. "Listen, luv, I gotta go start shootin' this thang, I'm already 45-minutes behind schedule. You're welcome to stay if you like?"

"Thanks. I just came with one of my girlfriends who's in the shoot", I said, trying not to be a groupie.

"Oh, yeah. Which one?"

"I'll show her to you", I said, as we exited the office and I witnessed Brea suspiciously leaving the area where Tonika's bags were. I pretended not to see her right away, so that she'd be back by her own stuff when I pointed her out. "Her name's Brea. There she is, right over there"

"Oh she's gorgeous. I'ma take care of her for you Jaz", D-Flava volunteered as though we were cool like that.

"And I'll make sure that B-wood calls you, too", I returned like I had pull like that.

"Do that!", he said as he went to the set.

I smiled as I made my way towards Brea, zig-zag-ing a path through dancers sprawled-out and stretching in preparation for the shoot.

"Brea, I'on't know what you were doing by that girl's bags, but I hope you ain't fucked nothin' up", I said in a hurried whisper voice.

"Quit trippin'! I said I had this under control", she said calmly but looking every bit guilty at my revealing that I'd seen her.

"I was talkin' with D-Flava, the director and told him that I was with Twisted Records and that I had a friend dancing today and he asked who, so I pointed you out and he said he's gonna take care of you", I spat out without taking a breath.

"Whaaatt?", Brea seemed shocked.

"He's also got a movie he's doing and he wants me to have Brandon call him, so I sang for him and he loved it, so hopefully, I might get on the soundtrack", I couldn't slow down.

"See, didn't I tell you that coming today would be a good thing?", Brea wrestled some of the credit for the good fortune I created. "Jaz, they're calling us over for instructions, I'll talk to you some more, when we get done"

"I might not stay", I said to Brea as she was quickly walking to the set, trying to make sure she'd be in the front during instructions.

I left about 45-minutes later. But I'd stayed long enough to witness, Tonika unexpectedly vomiting after drinking from her water bottle.

I shook my head out of pity, even not knowing the specific details of what Brea had done. But I knew she must've put something in Tonika's water to have her throwing-up and unable to dance in the video today.

Chapter Fifteen

On what was an extraordinarily beautiful Friday in the month of May, I received a disturbing phone call.

"Hello"

"Jazmyn, it's mom"

My mom spoke sounding somewhat distressed.

"What's wrong?", I immediately questioned, not able to get the answer fast enough.

"It's Tyisha. She's actin' all fast again and your dad's gonna kill her", mom said with urgency.

"What happened? Where's Dad? Where's Tyisha?", I rattled an on-slaught of questions.

"Tyisha's gettin' calls from grown-ass men again.

Your father's on his way home. I'm scared what your father might do", mom confided in me.

I was afraid too, 'cause I knew that my dad didn't play with shit like that. And, because of the fact that my mom called me for help, which she'd never do unless the situation was extremely serious. Not to mention that she actually cursed during her explanation.

"What'cha want me to do, mom?", I asked quickly, mindful of time because dad was already on his way home.

"Can you take your sister with you for a while? Just 'til things calm down", she asked.

"I'm on my way. Tell her to get her things packed. We'll pick-up more tomorrow while dad's at work", I suggested, as I raced out of my apartment like a fire-fighter to the scene of the 9/11 emergency.

I knew if I didn't get there fast, it would be too late for Tyisha and she'd be crumbling down, just as hard and fast as the Twin Towers.

I was pissed-off at Tyisha, who was now 17 and had just finished her junior year in high school, as I weaved through traffic on I-20.

Also, I thought about how it was a good thing that Brea had just moved-out earlier this month. Otherwise, it would've been real crowded in the apartment, especially seeing as I had no idea of how long she'd be staying with me and Trina.

Trina didn't mind Tyisha staying with us. But I kinda knew she wouldn't.

Mom had been updating me over the past month about Tyisha's behavior. I just figured that it was a teenage phase that everyone went through.

Tyisha was my little sister, but in age only. She was now an inch taller than me, had C-cup breasts that seemed to be nearing Brea-size and a butt that was closer to Trina's than mine.

With the exception of her baby-fat face, everything about her looked full-grown. But she wasn't.

I made it to the house before dad got back. And just by talking with Tyisha during the drive back to my apartment made me appreciate my mom and feel guilty for what I must've put my mother through when I was her age.

The next day, on Saturday morning, I took my car to get a badly-needed oil change. As I returned to my apartment building, I saw a girl that looked like Tyisha walking back into the building with Alantra, a girl about the same age as Tyisha, that lived in a neighboring apartment unit.

I parked my car and hurried to my apartment.

As I opened the door, I saw Trina in the kitchen making a sandwich. When Trina saw me, she had an uneasy expression on her face that clearly conveyed to me that it was indeed Tyisha that I'd seen.

"Tyisha!", I called her name.

She was in my bedroom.

"What, Jaz?", she said coming out of my room wearing a white tank top and some ultra-short shorts.

"Where'd you just go?", I interrogated.

"I just went to the store, dang", she grunted.

"Alright, first of all, you betta change the way you talk to me", I warned her. "You ASK me, if you can go to the store. You don't just leave"

"Ohh-kay", she whined back, as she turned to go back into my bedroom.

"Hold on just a minute!", I said, causing her to spin back around. "You went to the store wearing that?!"

"Whaaat? It's just shorts and a t-shirt", she prematurely started defending her inappropriate attire.

Trina's lips folded-in and her eyebrows raised like she'd already warned Tyisha that I would be mad if I caught her in that outfit.

"Okay, now YOU trippin'! I see that you done lost your damn mind!", I said.

The shorts she had on were so skimpy that you could see the bottom of her butt-cheeks and the white muscle tank top was stretched from her endowment so much that you could see the side of her breast through the arm hole.

Making it worse was that she didn't have on a bra and her partially erect nipples were poking and shining through her t-shirt like high-beam headlights on a car.

"It's hot…..", she began to start a bullshit excuse.

"I'on't even wanna hear it. That's some shit you wear to bed, not to the store. You ain't even got a bra on and I can see your damn nipples", I said loudly.

Tyisha's head tilted out of embarrassment of my comments in front of Trina, but I didn't care.

"Oh, don't act all shame now. You went all the way to the store not caring who was looking at your nipples, so don't act shame now!", I repeated my comments to purposely make her feel more uncomfortable.

Trina was trying to quickly finish her sandwich-making so that she'd be able to exit into her own room.

"You can't even see nothin'.....", Tyisha again attempted another bullshit justification, while looking down the front of her shirt like she didn't already know the outline of them were visible.

"Save it! This is a bra-wearing house. I don't give a damn if you think it's too hot! Then keep yo' ass inside. But from now on, you always wear a bra. Don't nobody wanna see you nipples and shit! I don't! And I'm sure Trina don't!", I laid down the law, sounding like my mother.

I hated to involve Trina, but it was true. Tyisha had to learn that just because she was my sister, didn't mean that other people would have to be tolerant of her bullshit.

I could already tell, no matter how much of the summer that Tyisha stayed, she was going to be work for me.

During all of the following week, I would drop Tyisha off at the Frederick Douglas Teen-Summer Camp held at a nearby YMCA as a way to keep her time occupied when I wasn't around and while I was at work. There was mega-supervision at the camp and kids weren't allowed to leave until the end of the day at 3:30 PM.

Normally, I'd still be at work when camp was over, so Tyisha would sometimes have to catch the bus back to the apartment.

The good thing was that it was Trina's last week of school at Spellman, so she was usually out of class by the time Tyisha got to the apartment. Because Trina was so smart, she didn't need a lot of study time and was able to help look-after Tyisha until I got home. It was sort-of parenting-by-committee.

I appreciated Trina's willingness to help me out.

My singing career also began looking bright, as Brandon decided to put Chocolate Cream into high-gear after speaking with D-Flava about the movie soundtrack.

Unfortunately, it meant spending late-nights at the studio, which caused me to rely more on Trina's baby-sitting of my sister than what I felt was fair to ask of a friend. But Trina never made me feel bad about it.

We'd recorded a couple of songs during that week and Brandon had even secured us a gig on Saturday night at the Champagne Room club in Roswell, Georgia. It was the kinda place where big name stars played.

I was excited and nervous. Things had moved so fast, that it had me doubting whether or not we were ready.

It made me glad that Simeon was going to be there to support me.

"How you doing, baby?", Simeon greeted me backstage with a hug shortly before we were to perform.

I showed him my shaking hand, as my answer.

"Don't worry, they're gonna love you!", Simeon encouraged.

"I hope so", I returned nervously.

I'd waited for this opportunity for what seemed like

an eternity, although in actuality it'd been less than a year, but now that it was here, I was scared.

I wished that my girls could've been here too, but Trina was at home with Tyisha and Brea was at an evening-scene video shoot.

The M.C. introduced us like we were established stars, "Here they are, the hottest up-n-coming group reppin' the A-T-L, Champagne Room make some noise for CHOCOLATE CREAM!!!"

I stayed back stage singing the hook to one of our new songs, "Lay-tah (Later)", as each member made it to the stage one by one as their parts came up. This entrance technique was taught to us by Brandon.

When I danced my way onto the stage last, as the only female in the group, I couldn't believe the roar that came from the crowd.

It was just what I needed to keep the nervousness out of my vocals.

The crowd was feelin' us and I utilized that energy to belt the hooks in between the other member's rap parts of the song.

"Watcha goin' do wit me Lay-tah", I seductively sang the hook, as I flirted with me eyes and my body to guys that were closest to the stage.

At the end of our four songs that we'd been allotted to perform, the crowd's reactions made the wait, worthwhile.

I'd never felt a high before like the one I just experienced after getting off stage.

All four of us in the group were jumpin' around like we lost our damn minds because we knew we'd just killed.

Tonight's success was an instant unifier, as none of us really knew much about each other. We were individual artist pulled together by Brandon.

"Alright, calm down! Calm down!", Brandon said to us backstage. "Y'all were great, but calm down and act like you've been here before"

His words did little to calm our reactions as we were rightfully excited. However, we did subdue our emotions long-enough to hear that he had good news. An Entertainment Reporter for *Rolling Out Magazine* was in the audience and was so impressed that he wanted to do a feature on the group.

Rolling Out is one of the top urban magazines distributed in major cities all over the country. A feature in a magazine like that was almost a guarantee that we'd hit the big time.

I gave the good news from backstage on my cell phone to my mom, Trina and left a message for Brea on her cell phone.

My dad still wasn't in support of my career choice, but my mom always wanted to hear the good news and would relay to my dad whether he wanted to hear it or not.

Part of my fuel and resolve to make it in the music business was to prove my father wrong, but it hadn't started out that way.

When I made my way from backstage into the club to meet-up with Simeon, people were congratulating me and complimenting me. Even one person wasn't shame to ask for my autograph – my first autograph.

"You were outstanding!", Simeon greeted me with a huge hug.

I noticed during my hug that I was getting major attention from all the fellas in the club. Almost Brea-like attention and it felt good.

Simeon had a surprise planned for me as a celebration. A late dinner and a hotel room at the luxurious Westin.

I called Trina to let her know of the unexpected plans and asked if she minded that I wouldn't be back until the next day. She didn't care because she had no plans for tonight. I wanted to make sure she'd be around the house with Tyisha.

Simeon and I had the most romantic night since we'd known each other. We sipped champagne in our suite, recapped the night's events until it was old and had raw-hot sex.

Simeon's tongue worked me so well that I wanted to get it bronzed.

"Ummmmm, ummmm, ummmm", I moaned as my legs shivered from his pleasurable licking.

His tongue varied pace of flicking, rolling and sucking and had my pussy dripping and on fire.

Twice I tried to escape, but Simeon refused to stop sucking my pussy until he had made me cum. He was freakier than I expected, as he tugged on my pussy lips with his mouth and occasionally lightly spanked my pussy with his hand.

"Ooooh, Ahhhh, OOOH-WOOO, Ahhh, OOOOH, AHHHHHHHHHHH!", I helplessly screamed as Simeon had two fingers churning deep in me with one hand, while the other hand was fanning back-n-forth across my clit faster than windshield wipers set on the highest setting.

My body jerked and contracted all over the place as my orgasm released onto his fingers. It seemed like it took 10-minutes for me to regain control of my eyeballs.

Though I tried to return the favor by giving mouth-love to his dick, Simeon chose to forgo the reciprocity because he was ready to fuck.

While Simeon rolled on a *Magnum* condom, I lied on my back, as he then raised my legs. Simeon's dick circumference filled me so tightly I had to pull my legs back towards my chest to make it easier for him to get inside.

Simeon had already made me so hot that from his first strokes I was already cumming again.

"Mmmmmmmm, mmmmmmmm, mmmmm", I groaned with folded-in lips, trying to endure.

"Howzit feel, baby?", Simeon's deep voice enchanted.

I wasn't good at the bed talk, especially while I was being fucked well. So well, that I feared unfolding my lips to speak would make me lose total control.

"Jazmyn, howzit feel, baby??!", Simeon repeated.

"Good. Good.", finally I simply responded, not wanting to lose too much of my concentration.

"Just good? Oh, I gotta do better than that! I want it to be great!", Simeon commented before up-ing his pace and depth.

Simeon's deep pounding unlocked my folded lips.

"Mmmmm-Ahhhh SHIT! Uhnnnn-SHIT! OOOOH SHIT!", I cried out at the taking of the most dick I'd ever had in my entire life.

"Howzit now? Jazymn, howzit now?", he commanded an answer.

All I could answer with was more intense moans of passion, but that wasn't satisfactory.

"HOW IS IT?! I'ma give you MORE if you don't answer!", Simeon seductively threatened.

"Uhnnn-IT'S GREAT!! Simeon, IT'S GREAT!!", I yelled before he made good on his promise and gave me all twelve inches of him.

"That's what I'm talkin' about!", he said confidently as he turned me over.

While I was on my hands and knees, he moved my legs together and entered from the back. My legs being pushed together made his dick fit even tighter in my pussy.

Simeon gripped my butt firmly with his hands and gradually released his grip, all the while keeping a steady stroking pace that had me biting on the sheets.

Next, Simeon straddled directly over my butt and pushed on the back of my shoulders until my torso and head was flat on the bed.

My body was now in the triangle position of a take-off ramp with my butt being the top of the ramp.

As he continued thrusting from this angle, he had gravity on his side as each pump dropped in me from a perfectly vertical position.

"Oooo, baby. Your pussy feels so good!", I heard Simeon grunt, as I could feel his dick throbbing in me.

Simeon's dick was so firm and felt so good that I almost wanted to cry. He'd given me a personal-record six orgasms, evenly distributed, three in each position.

My feet kicked the bed with each stroke until I felt Simeon remove himself from me, strip his condom off and let his warm manhood cascade down my back.

I reached behind me with one hand to grab-hold of his still throbbing thang and stroked all of his manhood out of him. With the other hand, I rubbed my pussy as it immediately became lonely from the absence of his dick in it.

Both of our sweaty and out-of-breath bodies rested next to each other, staring at the ceiling from exhaustion.

Just like the wait to get a chance in the music business was appearing to be worthwhile, so had this moment Simeon and I just shared. Our first time together was full of pent-up passion that'd been delayed too long. Yet and still, it was the deferrals that made the timing now perfect. The moment, pure.

Later, we took a shower together before I lied in Simeon's arms to fall asleep and learned the true meaning of complete peace of the mind, soul and spirit.

Chapter Sixteen

"Hello? Hello? Hell—lll-oohh?", I answered the phone at a little after 8:00 AM on Tuesday morning.

"Is Brea home?", the ominous man's voice asked.

"Brea don't live here anymore", I said frustrated while looking at the Caller-I.D. to see that it was yet another call for Brea from a 718-area code.

"Where she live now?!", the mysterious man said, as though it was a demand, in an east-coast accent.

"WHO IS THIS?!", I whipped back.

Click. The phone hung-up, as I scowled at the receiver with a disdained look upon my face.

"Who was that, another call for Brea?", Trina asked.

"Yeah. Sometime this week, we goin' have to get our

number changed", I informed Trina.

Over the past four days, we'd gotten so many calls for Brea from men that didn't wanna leave their names or a message. Most of them from the same NYC, 718-area code.

"Was it that 718-number, again?", Trina inquired, stirring her cup of coffee.

"Yeah. I'on't know who he is, but Brea must've fucked the shit out of him or something 'cause he wanna get back in touch with her bad!", I laughed to Trina.

"I know!", Trina added, "He sounds like a white boy too!"

"You know, I was thinkin' the same thing, but I didn't say nothing 'cause I wasn't sure if it was that New York accent that was throwin' me off or not", I commented back.

Trina was in the midst of Final Exams Week at Spellman. Other than an extra cup of coffee in the morning, she never showed any signs of stressing about them. That definitely wasn't the case for me and Brea back when we were still in school.

"Tyisha! Hurry up!", I yelled at my sister's slow-poking around in the bathroom.

I had a busy day today and she was gonna mess-up my schedule with her teenage-ish overly-concerned prepping in the bathroom.

I had to drop her off at camp, go by Twisted's studio in Stone Mountain to lay down some vocals on a couple of new songs for Brandon that would be submitted for review for the movie soundtrack and still make it to work at *Reflex* by at least 11:45, 'cause I had a Noon-appointment scheduled.

Even after work, I had to go back to the studio for a short rehearsal from 5:00-6:00 PM because Brandon had secured another last-minute gig.

"Tyisha, do you have your key to the apartment?", I asked, sitting in the car in front of the Summer Camp.

"Yes! You asked me that three times already", she responded irritated.

"Let me see it", I demanded proof.

"See-eee", she pulled it out of her purse.

"Okay, okay. I just wanted to make sure!", I explained my over-zealousness. "I gotta go to the studio tonight until 6 o'clock and Trina's gonna be in class taking Finals. So, you're gonna catch the bus home. Bring yo' ass straight home! I'ma call you to make sure!", I aggressively informed her.

"I know, danggggg! I always come straight home!", she said.

And Tyisha was speaking the truth. Since she'd been staying with us, she'd never failed to come straight home on the bus. I was just nervous because this time, Trina was gonna be in class and not already home, expecting her arrival.

As I drove to Twisted's studios, I hated that I had to record vocals so early. I worried about how well my singing would be, 'cause I figured, nobody sounds good in the morning.

Partially because of Tyisha's primpin' in the bathroom and our car conversation, I was 20-minutes late when I arrived. And I knew that word would get back to Brandon later in the day about me wasting money by having recording engineers waiting for me.

To my surprise, when I got there, Brandon was sitting in the booth.

"I know. I know, Brandon – I'm late. I had to drop-off my younger sister at camp", I spoke, not waiting for him to complain before I began my excuse, as I rushed to set my bag down on the floor.

"What do I always say?", Brandon pressed the intercom button and asked me to repeat his motto from behind the glass window that separated the engineering room and the recording studio.

"If a singer ain't ate, they were probably late", I unenthusiastically humored him by showing him that I remembered his line.

"That's right! Remember that!", he said.

His motto referred to his account that most 'Starving Artist' are only starving because they're always late and as a reminder of his policy that if this had been a performance gig, I wouldn't be paid because I was late.

Thankfully he let it go, as he motioned to the engineer to give me the music sheets for the songs.

I sat on the stool in front of the microphone, bobbing my head to the instrumental track the engineer was playing that we were going to record over, and looked over the lyric-sheets.

About 2-hours later, we'd finished what I came to do and I was busy calling Sumy to let her know that I was gonna be about 40-minutes late coming in to *Reflex* and she wasn't very happy with me either.

"Jazmyn, let me holla at you for a minute", Brandon motioned me into his office.

"Can you just yell at me later? I'ma be late again at my other job", I informed him.

"It'll just take a minute", he said with urgency.

I sighed frustration, yet followed him into his office.

"What's up?", I said, not even sitting down to show that I really didn't have time for the tongue-lashing that I thought he'd called me into his office for.

"I've decided that we're gonna add another female singer to balance out the group", he just came right-out and said.

"What?! Just 'cause I was a little late today?", I sternly questioned.

"No it's not that. Right now, you're the only female in the group with three male rappers. I just think it would be best for the group to have another female singer in the group with you for balance-sake. It'll look better on stage and add a little more flava", Brandon continued.

I hated the idea. Had tons of questions and rebuttals, but I also had to get to work.

"You just want more sex-appeal, huh?", I tried to extract clues to his rationale.

"Truthfully, YEAH! That's part of it, but not all of it", he wasn't ashamed to admit.

"Who is she?", I asked, suspicious of whether or not

she even could sing, or if she'd gotten this opportunity due to some horizontal talents she'd shown to Brandon.

"You'll meet her tonight at rehearsal", he said coyly.

"Oh, it's like that? The group doesn't get to vote?", I sarcastically questioned, looking at my watch.

"Jaz, chill. Don't mess-up! Chocolate Cream is my group! I put y'all together!", he said standing up.

"Whattabout the songs we've already recorded?.... Nevermind, I gotta go!", I abruptly ended our conversation by storming off.

When I got to work at *Reflex*, I let off some steam by telling Brea about what had occurred.

"Fuck Brandon! If he can't appreciate you, then FUCK 'EM!", Brea charged. "Besides, you're the one that told him about the movie soundtrack thing!"

Brea was a good sounding board, but only while silent. Whenever she opened her mouth, her ghetto-ness ended-up proving the opposite point of what she was saying. And in this case, the opposite of what I wanted to acknowledge.

I'd only given Brandon a message from D-Flava about the movie soundtrack. Even if I hadn't, I'm sure D-Flava would've contacted Brandon anyway. And it was true that he'd formed the group and invested in it, so what could I really say about anything.

Truth be known, I was just tired. Tired of being told that I wasn't sexy enough to sell records as a solo artist by

Joseph Myer's label execs in New York. And now, it was basically the same thing with Brandon.

It was very discouraging that whenever things seemed to be going right with my career, there was always something that would come-up.

This time, I decided that I'd just have to tough-it-out and not ruin it for myself because I was closer than I'd ever been to my goal of becoming a star.

Plus, I wasn't planning on taking any advice from Brea. She was my girl and all, but she was also the one that'd gotten herself kicked-off the Atlanta Hawks cheerleading team.

It was bothering me all day at *Reflex* that Trina had Finals to take at Spellman and wouldn't be home by the time Tyisha arrived from summer-camp.

Making it worse was that I had a good-tipping client that was scheduled to come in today from 3:00 to 4:00, leaving me just enough time, to get to the studio on-time at 5 PM.

It was a tough decision, but I decided to reschedule my 3:00 PM appointment to another day, so that I'd be able to leave *Reflex* early and stop by the apartment before I had to go to the studio.

I finished my 2:00 o'clock appointment around 2:30 PM, lied to an already upset Sumy, saying that I had an emergency and was out the door at 2:45 PM.

Traffic on I-285 was crazy. It was 3:45 PM when I was finally turning the key to open my front door.

I was absolutely frozen stiff by what I saw.

Tyisha was butt-ass naked on the pull-out sofa bed with her hands on the back rest passionately screaming while he was gripping the shit out of her titties and fucking her, doggie-style.

It wasn't until they became aware of my presence, as they each turned their head in my direction, before I finally snapped out of my temporary daze. And snapped, is exactly what I did.

As if it weren't enough to catch my under-age sister fuckin' someone in my own apartment, seeing and already knowing the man delivering the pumps made me temporarily insane.

"Are you out of your FUCKING mind!!", I slammed my purse down and screamed loud enough to strain my own voice.

"Hey…ahh….Jazmyn look I …. Uhh..", he stuttered.

"She's 17, Jamal! SEVENTEEN!! I should call the fuckin' police on yo' ass! GET… THE FUCK OUT…MY HOUSE… RIGHT NOW!!", I yelled as I stalked his naked body around the bed, armed with a vase in my hand.

"She said that she was 18!", Jamal shouted nervously, as he tried to explain the unexplainable.

"Jazmyn….", Tyisha had the nerve to say my name.

"You SHUT THE FUCK UP!", I howled at her, raising the vase, threatening to hit her with it. "Don't you say ANOTHER FUCKIN' WORD TO ME!"

Jamal had utilized the time when my attention had been distracted towards Tyisha to retrieve his underwear and pants.

"I should fuckin' kill you!", I berated at Jamal, as I

continued my pursuit of him around the pull-out sofa bed.

"Jazmyn, I SWEAR! She told me that she was 18!", he continued pleading his case for me not to call the police.

"FUCK YOU, JAMAL!!", I said as I lost it and threw the vase at him.

The vase broke as it hit him in the arm causing a bleeding cut. He didn't complain or show any inkling to retaliate, other than to sincerely try to convince me of his innocence, which was impossible and not dependant on what she'd said or not said.

"I'm sorry, Jaz! I'm sorry!", Jamal humbly apologized as he backed his way out of the front door.

Because I'd used my only weapon, I didn't pursue him.

Tyisha was crying and shaking with nervousness, seeing me in a state she'd never witnessed before.

"Jaz-azz-myn-nn-nn", she sniffled my name.

"Take yo' ass to my room and get fuckin' dressed!", I demanded to her.

Up until that moment, my anger had made me ignore her nudity. Though I wasn't finished with her, not even close, I wasn't gonna continue while lookin' at her bare titties and ass.

While she was getting dressed and thunderously sobbing in my room, I sprayed damn near an entire can of Lysol until it was empty and my eyes were stinging. All in an attempt to remove even the slightest hint of Jamal and my sister's sex aroma from my nostrils.

There was a knock at the door by a concerned apartment-neighbor that heard all of the shouting. I eased their concern by telling them that everything was okay--it was just an argument that got settled, so there was no need to call the police. I just preferred keepin' family business private.

"It don't take that long to put your fuckin' clothes back on! Come out here!", I renewed my screaming at Tyisha.

I knew Tyisha was scared to come back out and face me, which she should've been.

Tyisha entered the room with watery eyes and her head hanging, but it didn't cause me to pity her.

"Why you tryin' to act like a fuckin' hoe?!", I just picked a place to start out of the many issues I had with her.

It was everything that pissed me off. Her age. Fuckin' at my place. Jamal's age. Fuckin' someone she didn't even know like a hoe. Everything.

She didn't dare answer and rightfully so, 'cause there was nothing she could say that wouldn't send me off the deep-end again.

Time had renewed my brain to at least some sort of sanity, as I began thinking about more than just expressing my rage.

"Are you hurt?!", I questioned, while possessing a contradicting face that looked nothing like concern.

"No", Tyisha meekly mumbled back.

"I mean ... he didn't hurt you, did he?", I again asked. This time trying to soften my question, so that I could have faith in her answer.

"No, he didn't hit me or nothing", she responded, showing her age.

"I ain't talkin' about that. I'm talking about, did he

hurt you down there?", I clarified to my sister's young ass by having to point to the area.

"Ohhh! Ohhh! No", she said, as her face showed that she now understood what I meant.

"I'm serious about this. If you're hurt, let me know Tyisha!", I said sternly.

"I'm not hurt. I'm fine."

I knew what Jamal had and I wasn't sure of my sister's level of sexual experience, which I obviously hoped wasn't much, but I just wanted to make sure of whether or not we needed to go see a doctor.

At the moment I walked through the door, I was angry enough that I could've actually killed Jamal.

Several minutes removed, I think I still could've killed him, but it pained me to acknowledge some wrong-doing that was not on his part. I knew part of the problem rested with my sister's lying to him about her age.

I thought about calling Simeon to have him kick Jamal's ass, which I knew he would do over a situation like this. At the same time, I was embarrassed as hell over my sister's behavior and didn't want anyone to know. Not my mom, not Simeon, not Trina nor Brea.

The heat from my anger built-up in me until it had given me a severe headache and my eyes were blood-shot red.

I hated to do it, especially after the drama this morning, but I called-in to Twisted studios to let them know that I wasn't gonna be at rehearsal tonight.

Chapter Seventeen

When Trina got home, I left my apartment. I just had to get out of there. I was about to lose my damn mind and just needed to be some place else.

I didn't tell Trina what was going on. I just told her that if she planned to leave to call me and I'd come right back home.

After a long day of Final Exams, Trina wasn't planning to go anywhere.

I drove around the I-285 loop twice, before I decided to stop by *Slick-N-Thick* to hang-out with Brea, who was working tonight and always good for a laugh.

The club wasn't as busy as on the weekends, yet I was still surprised at the number of people in the club on a Tuesday night.

I sat at the bar, as I couldn't see Brea anywhere. I figured that she must be in the back-room changing or something.

It did feel different going to the club alone and without Trina. I found myself turning down dancers that must've assumed that I was a lesbian, as different women kept coming up to me to ask if I'd like a lap-dance.

After about 15-minutes, I was getting frustrated waiting to see Brea, but I knew she was here, at least that's what the last two dancers that had come-up to me said when I asked.

I was debating whether or not to order another drink, or should I just leave, when I saw Brea coming out of one of the VIP-rooms. She was laughing to someone that was hidden by the corridor wall that led to the VIP-rooms.

Seeing that at least she was here, I turned my attention to the bartender to order the drink I'd previously debated.

It took a few minutes to get the bartender's attention and when I turned back around, I didn't see Brea anymore.

Damn! Just great!, I thought to myself.

I scanned the room for her. Eventually I located her. She had her back to me, grinding on a customer that was seated in a chair.

It's a damn shame that I'm able to recognize her from the back, I thought.

I wasn't gonna interrupt her during her dancing, but I wanted to walk past her, so that she'd know that I was here.

As I attempted to do so, I was already beginning to gain my laughter from Brea, as her legs straddled the seated man whose face was blocked by Brea's gyrating body. Brea held onto the back of the chair behind the man's head and had her titties all up in his face.

I sped-up my walk, as I wanted for her to notice me while she was doing that shit because I knew her reaction was sure to make me smile.

Boy, was I ever wrong. When Brea saw me she did smile, but when she moved the giant titty of hers that blocked the man's face to reveal it was Mr. Whitfield that she was dancing for, I lost my smile.

"Heyy-aaayy … umm … umm …", Mr. Whitfield struggled to recall my name as he was very drunk.

"Jazymn!", Brea helped him remember my name.

I was embarrassed as hell. For him. For me being in the club in front of him. For Brea working in the club. For the fact that she'd had her titties all in his face. I didn't know what to do.

Brea and Mr. Whitfield seemed not to be uncomfortable at all.

I know my face had an *Eeewww* expression on it witnessing a friend of mine's father in this state.

"Jazmyn, join us!", Mr. Whitfield invited me. "You want a drink?"

"No thank you", I politely responded with my feet glued to the floor.

"Sit down, Jazmyn", he encouraged pulling out a chair as Brea continued grinding to the beat of the song.

"I …. I … um ….", I stumbled like a eight-year old child that was in trouble.

Brea seemed to be enjoying my discomfort, as she had a huge grin across her face as I struggled.

215

"Oh, relax Jazmyn. We're all grown folks. You already know that Mrs. Whitfield and I are getting a divorce. Ain't nothing wrong going on here. It's cool. I'm just having some fun. Please, sit down", Mr. Whitfield explained and again offered, tapping on the chair he'd pulled out.

I slid cautiously into the chair and sat upright like I was in elementary school.

"Hey-aayyy!", Brea sang raising one hand in the air at the start of Ludacris' song '*Move*'.

The alcohol on Mr. Whitfield was so intense, I feared anyone around lighting a cigarette.

"Do you work here too?", Mr. Whitfield questioned like he was gonna come back on the day I worked to see me naked.

"NO!", I emphatically said, as though I'd been asked if I'd committed a murder and louder than I intended.

With my stern and adamant denial, I'd accidentally insulted Brea. But I later thought, *Shit, Brea don't give a damn anyway*, and obviously wasn't offended as she continued squeezing her titties with both hands in Mr. Whitfield's face like she was trying to squirt him with milk.

"Brea, what in the hell are you doing?", I asked to her while Mr. Whitfield was in the bathroom, but not with the enthusiasm I'd normally have if I'd not already had such a horrible day.

It was *de ja vu* all over again, just like the deal with her and Jamal, except this time it was much more serious 'cause it was Trina's dad.

"Whatcha mean? Oh, don't start trippin'! I WORK HERE! Micheal came here! I'm just doing my job! I'on't turn nuthin' down but my shirt collar!", Brea defended the awkward situation.

I was emotionally exhausted. So, I was like *'Fuck It'*. As far as I was concerned, this shit was between Brea, Mr. Whitfiled and Trina, if she ever found out.

"Well---ll? I guess, that's up to y'all", I sighed.

My decision to not emotionally invest in this situation made me relax more.

It was becoming more clear to me that I had an unrealistic view of the world and what people should do.

"Jaz, Micheal is one of the best customers I've ever had! I done already made $400 from him!", she was excited to brag like he was one of her normal suckers.

I was shocked that he'd be throwing money around like that to her 'cause the info I had from Trina was that both of her parents were strapped for cash because of their frozen accounts.

"I'on't know where he's getting that money from?", I said to Brea 'cause she knew the story about the frozen accounts as well.

"Don't believe everything you hear. Michael's got a secret stash of money that Mrs. Whitfield doesn't know about!", Brea explained information she must've gotten from the drunken and defenseless Mr. Whitfield.

I just shook my head.

The next mid-morning, my head-shaking continued as I stopped by Brea's apartment to pick-up the small wallet-purse I'd carried into the club the night before and left sitting right on the table.

I was always forgetting that thing because it was so tiny and easy to forget. But at the same time I liked the convenience, when I just needed my I.D. and a few dollars.

Brea *shushed* me as I entered her apartment and later I'd be grateful that she did.

During my brief visit I'd learned that she'd taken Mr. Whitfield home with her and he was still asleep in her bed.

I didn't even allow Brea's ghetto-ass a chance to disclose details, as she was trying to brag about being able to hook an older debonair man. Instead, I left in a hurry, not wanting to accidentally hear more information or risk Mr. Whitfield knowing that I knew about it.

In the evening, I arrived at Twisted Records around 6:20 PM for our 7:00 rehearsal, not really giving a damn about what anyone would have to say to me about missing yesterday's rehearsal.

I was actually 40-minutes early today, as Trina was back from Spellman and at the apartment with Tyisha. I was still pissed-off and couldn't stand looking at Tyisha longer than I had to, so I left earlier than needed.

Shanay, Twisted's ghetto-hoochie receptionist raised her eyes when she saw me enter like she knew that I was gonna be in trouble.

I just ignored her antics as I walked past, 'cause I really didn't give a shit.

"Jazmyn!", I heard Brandon yell for me from his office across the hall, loud enough for everyone in the office to hear.

"Yes?!", I turned around with attitude of my own.

"I need to talk with you!....NOW!", he dictated.

"What, Brandon?!", I said, not in the mood.

"You betta whatch that attitude with me!"

"Brandon, honestly I'm not in the mood right now!", I stood-up to him.

"I don't give a fuck what you're in the mood for! We had rehearsal last night and you weren't here!"

"I had personal shit to take care of. I called-in", I limited my explanation.

"There's nothing more important than the group! What'd you have to do that was important enough to miss rehearsal?!", Brandon claimed.

"You know what, Brandon? My personal shit ain't none of your business. You don't have to believe me if you don't fuckin' want to, I don't give a damn, but I'm tired and can't take this shit!", I said, as I started to shiver and was feeling like I was on the verge of a nervous breakdown.

I could tell that Brandon could see that there was more going-on with me than just some irresponsibility, as his eyes softened and he now closed the door for privacy. I think he felt a little guilty for assuming.

"Have a seat, Jazmyn", Brandon now offered courteously. "Look, I'm sorry for whatever is going-on in your life. I truly am. If you need some time off…."

"No, I'm cool", I jumped in.

"Okay, Jazmyn. But you gotta understand that I'm

running a business. Plus, it ain't fair to the other members that show up. So, the bottom line is that I can't have anymore of this. Are you cool with that?"

"Yeah", I said, actually meaning it.

I was tired of drama or worrying about drama. Sitting in Brandon's chair I had made up my mind that I was going to put everything into my music and wouldn't let any drama stop me. Not my sister's, not Trina's, not Brea's, not my parents', nobody's!

My decision was made not to make Brandon happy, but it was totally for me. Singing was where I found real joy.

We finished our meeting and when I went into the recording studio my new found resolve would be tested immediately, as I met for the first time the new female singer in the group. It was Tonika, the dancer that Brea had *'poisoned'* at the video shoot.

Immediately, I knew that Brandon probably had plans to make her a focal point more than me if she even had at least an average voice.

Shemar, Jerome and Khalid were already smitten by her good looks, as they were hovering around her like she was gold or something, as I walked in.

I really didn't have anything against her. And after rehearsal was over, I knew that it was Brea that was just jealous, as Tonika didn't act like she was all that.

Clearly, I was the better singer, but she had a nice voice too.

My previous innocence and naivety had been stripped clean by everything that was going-on around me.

I hated to admit it, but my thought process was quickly becoming more like Brea's and it wasn't all bad. It was just about reaching my goals.

Knowing that we had the soundtrack thing coming up, which now included a small role in the movie itself, I wasn't gonna allow myself to be pushed out of the lime-light by Tonika, whether I liked her or not.

During the rehearsal of some new songs, I noticed the singing parts that were given to her were the better ones, despite my having the nicer voice.

I read the hand-writing on the wall, that this was being done for marketing purposes. The more lyrics she had meant more screen-time in an inevitable video of the group.

I was dead-set on not sitting idly-by and watch this occur. A move had to be made to prevent this before it went too far and I was prepared to make it.

Brea would've done something sinister to Tonika, but I wasn't that ghetto. Yet, that didn't mean that I wasn't as determined to get what I wanted. I was gonna fight fire with fire.

After rehearsal had ended, I purposely lingered around the studio for a couple of hours until only a few people remained.

I surprised Brandon in his office.

"Jazmyn? What are you still doing here?", he was genuinely surprised to see me.

"You'll see", I said aggressively, as I pulled the blinds on the window in his office.

"What's up, Jaz?", he said, curious as to why I'd done that.

I didn't speak another word to him, as I knelt before him and unzipped his pants and struggled with him to pull-out his dick.

"Jaz, I know you're feelin' something, but I don't know if you really wanna.....", he tried to say with conviction, but curtailed his comments when I had his dick in my hand.

It was a one-sided conversation, as I never responded to anything else he said as I continued.

What I was doing was the last thing he'd expect of me because he'd come to think of me as different from all the other women that hung around the studio.

"Ja-azzzz, don't....", he meekly whined like he wanted to keep me his good girl, but intrigued at the same time.

His whining was to no avail, as I wrapped my lips around him and gave him the best dick-sucking of his life. It was raw, raunchy and bold. Even sucked down his cum and everything.

When he finished shaking from his nut, I wiped some of his remaining juices that was on my face into my mouth with my fingers and spoke for the first time.

"I'ma ALWAYS be the #1 girl in this group!", I confidently spoke and smiled at him.

With that, I grabbed my bag and left him, limp-dick hangin'-out and all.

Chapter Eighteen

I had no idea how relieved I'd be in June when Tyisha moved back home with my parents. After just a few weeks with her, I didn't think that I'd ever wanna have kids.

Life was good for me. Brandon had renewed faith in me again and returned me to being the lead singer for Chocolate Cream.

In about a week from today, the band would be going to Los Angeles for the filming of the movie. Our role was small, just a short cameo-scene where we'd be the band playing at a night club in the background during one of the scenes, but it was still exposure. Even though the clip of the band would only be about 15-seconds in the movie, as the lead singer, I'd get the most of the few seconds, so I was excited.

I'd wondered if my dick-sucking with Brandon would turn into a nightly ritual. I wasn't worried about it or nothin', 'cause I'd already made up my mind that whatever it took, I was gonna do it.

Surprisingly, it never turned into that. Brandon treated me with utmost respect, which I found attractive, especially knowing that he could've taken advantage of our situation. And because it was clear that he was no angel, but for some reason he made a point to not be thuggish with me.

Actually, we were becoming closer as we'd go out together after a recording session.

Brandon had spent some time in the penitentiary for attempted murder, which caught me off guard, as I never would've guessed that.

He wasn't completely reformed of that life-style, as he confessed that he was funding the studio from drug-dealing. But it seemed like his goal was to make the studio successful enough that he'd be able to leave the underground lifestyle alone completely, which I respected.

There was something captivating about Brandon being a bad-boy, yet wasn't so tough that he was against being able to smile and have fun. Plus, it seemed like he was truly taking an interest in me beyond the singing.

We'd just changed our home phone number a couple of days ago because we couldn't take all the hang-up calls we were getting, a left-over problem from Brea's residency. But the final straw was that we more frequently got calls from the same guy with the 718-area code number that was now insisting that Brea still lived at our apartment. He'd even call and say 'Hey Brea' to me or Trina when we'd answer, like maybe we were actually Brea and that we'd be fooled because it sounded like he knew us.

"I got us some passes to an exclusive party that Herman's throwing", Brea said proudly handing out the passes to me and Trina at work at *Reflex*.

From the moment I touched them, I could feel how expensive they felt. The paper was linen, with gold foil embroidery. The price on the passes was $150. The party was titled 'Wild Thangz' and was gonna be held at the Ritz Carlton Hotel in Buckhead.

Reflex and the studio had been consuming so much of my time that I was dying for a girls' night out.

On Friday, the night of the party, we rolled up in style in Brea's Mercedes dressed sexy as the stars we thought we were.

We signed the guest registry and wrote only our first names on the name tag they gave. I started not to put mine on, as it messed-up the look of my outfit.

Despite being at a regal hotel, it wasn't a formal affair, more of a club-ish style of dress. R&B music was being played by the DJ, as we mingled through the crowd of about 60 to 80 people that'd been invited.

"I wonder why they call this a 'Wild Thangz' party?", Trina expressed out loud.

I wondered the same thing, but I didn't care as they had one hell of a food-spread which included shrimp the size of my thumb. The food was free and so were the drinks.

For the three of us, we could tell that we'd walked into baller-heaven. Anyone could tell that, by all the diamond-n-platinum-bling that was worn on wrists and fingers. Everyone here had madd-loot.

Some of the men were here with women, but it was difficult to tell who was and who wasn't, as everyone mingled comfortably.

"What's up Herman?", Brea hugged Herman as he was passing by with a woman. "How you doin' Tyanna?", she added with a hug to her as well.

"I'm glad that you all could make it!", Herman said, including me and Trina.

Brea introduced us to Tyanna, who was Herman's wife that we never got to actually meet when we'd first gone to the strip-club, several months back.

Tyanna was Beyonce'-cute, with her thick-self. She had a great smile and golden-brown micro-braids.

It only took a few minutes to learn why Brea liked her boss' wife so much, 'cause she was just like her. The only difference was that Tyanna had real money, but judging by her style of speech, clearly she was one dedicated to keepin' it real.

I was shocked when Brea's ghetto-ass took Herman to the dance floor and even more by the fact that her action didn't cause a problem with Tyanna, as she just laughed.

"Is this y'alls first time at a 'Wild Thangz' party?", Tyanna asked.

"Yeah", we both responded feeling like we didn't belong because we didn't even know what it meant.

I think me and Trina were waiting for each other to ask, but neither one us did, not wanting to look stupid.

"Well, you know everything's free. So help yourself to some food and drinks!", Tyanna urged to make us comfortable before leaving to resume her hosting duties.

I couldn't put my finger on it, but something felt strange about the party. I didn't know exactly what it was though. I thought seeing so many rich folks being so down to earth might've been it.

The other parties that I'd gone to where rich black folks were present, always seemed boring and boogee. You know, where everyone is walking around trying to act more sophisticated than the next person. This party was precisely the opposite.

Trina, Brea and I weren't rich. And we did just what non-rich black folks did at events like this – made sure to take advantage of the free drinks and food.

By 2:00 AM, all three of us were drunk as hell and laughing at any little thing.

Most of the people at the party had rented rooms at the hotel, so they'd not have to drive home drunk.

"Look at her!", I nudged to Trina.

"Where?", she responded.

"That woman right over there, kissing that man. I could've sworn she came in here with that other guy, remember?", I commented.

"Girl, you're drunk!", Brea claimed. "And why you all up-in ev-ery-one's bizness, anyway?"

"Shit, you're drunk too", I stated, not denying my own intoxication–level. "How in the hell are we gonna get home?"

"All I need is a little coffee and then I'll be good-to-go", Brea tried to convince, as Herman and his wife walked up to us.

"Are you guys having a good time?", Herman asked.

"Yeah", we all responded.

"Did you guys rent a room at the hotel?", Tyanna questioned.

"Uhn-uhn", we responded.

"You guys aren't gonna drive home tonight, are you?", Herman questioned with concern.

"I'm-mmm cool-lll", Brea slurred, which proved that she wasn't. "I just need a little coffee, that's all."

Trina and I knew that she was lying, but weren't gonna bust her out in front of her bosses.

Tyanna leaned-over and whispered something to Herman.

"We got a suite with extra rooms. You can come up to our room and get some rest. Leave tomorrow or later tonight if you want", he suggested.

I know me and Trina were down for that, rather than ending-up as a drunk-driving statistic.

We waited as they went over to put someone in command of the party during their absence while they took us up to the suite. My eyes instinctively followed them, as they passed by a woman that was kissing another woman.

When we got up to the suite, it was gorgeous like the one I'd stayed-in while in New York. And, it felt good to be off of my feet when we plopped down on the sofa in the living room.

We didn't wanna seem rude by just heading straight to the extra bedroom, so we stayed and chatted with them for a while.

When Herman went into the bedroom to get something, Trina asked the question we'd all been curious about, "Why do you call this a 'Wild Thangz' party?"

"You mean, you guys don't know?", Tyanna was astonished.

"Uhn-uhn", I said, shaking my head.

"Well, it's a swingers-party", Tyanna plainly informed.

I was trippin', but now I knew why it felt different.

"Oh, snap! Are you for real?", Brea sat up and said, covering her mouth with one hand as Herman returned from the bedroom with a silver-tray full of what appeared to be cocaine.

My heart started racing at the site of the huge amount of drugs on the platter, as I had visions of being on the next episode of 'COPS'.

Brea was the first of the three of us to actually partake by snorting some of the cocaine and Trina followed. I'd never done cocaine in my life before, but I conceded to trying it.

Immediately after snorting it, I didn't feel any different like I thought I would. There was a delayed reaction. The high was kind-of a sneaky one, more of a foggy high. I found myself staring into space occasionally. And now, everything moved in slow motion and voices seemed echo-ee.

"Herman, they didn't know what a 'Wild Thangz' party was about", Tyanna laughed to her husband.

"Well, show them", Herman directed.

Tyanna sat next to Brea and began fondling her breast as she tongue-kissed her.

We were so high, we only laughed, as Tyanna wasted no time pulling up Brea's shirt, squeezing and caressing her titties, as Brea blushingly smiled. Because we knew Brea so well, her smile was a clear sign of nervousness, though she'd never admit it. And as expected, Brea responded aggressively by doing the same back to Tyanna.

Me and Trina laughed like cocaine-addicts, as Herman disappeared back into the bedroom and returned shortly armed with a wicker-basket filled with condoms and sex toys.

Immediately, Herman knelt in front of Trina, lifted her shirt and started nibbling her peaks before saying to Tyanna, "Hey babe, check these out", referring to her extremely long nipples. It wasn't long before he included me by doing the same.

"Mmmmmm!", I heard Brea moan, as I turned my head to the left to witness that Tyanna had removed Brea's top completely, slid off the mini skirt she had on and was busily rubbing her hand across her pussy.

"Herm, come here", Tyanna asked, as he did.

Herman scooped-up Brea's naked body from the sofa in his arms and laid her on the bear-skin rug in front of us. Tyanna knelt behind Brea's head, as her plump thighs provide a head-rest for her while Herman placed his face between Brea's legs.

"OOOH, OOOH, OOOH", Brea chanted at the very first licking by Herman, as Tyanna combed through Brea's hair with her fingers.

"You guys, come down here", Tyanna invited, as Herman looked-up to make sure that we were coming.

Tyanna directed us to each side of Brea, as Herman pulled off his pants and we got our first look at the massive package he possessed. He was a 'King Kong' indeed – every bit of the fourteen inches Brea'd heard about.

"Suck her tits", Tyanna directed for us to start doing.

I was high as hell, but still had some instincts about me, so I delayed a moment until I witnessed Trina bending down and Brea not caring. As I gripped her huge titty with both hands and put my mouth for the first time on a woman's titty, I hated to admit to myself that it didn't feel as unnatural as I'd always assumed that it would. Swirling my tongue around the nipple while feeling it harden, I now seemed to understand more why men are so intrigued by a woman's body. I could hear Brea's heating-up sounds, as me and Trina continued. Our gender didn't seem to matter, as it was the actions that created this effect.

Brea raised her head and had a worried look when Herman rejoined us, now wearing a condom. He placed Brea's legs on his shoulders and rubbed the tip of his thang up-n-down her slit, which had her occasionally jerking.

"OOOOH! OOOHOH! OOOOH!", Brea grunted at the initial entrance, as her head whipped back.

Herman's depth was only 3-inches, but his shit was so huge, I'm sure it felt like 50-feet. With my hands still cupping Brea's titty, I could feel the trembling of her body, as I saw her face squint. Trina resumed nipple-nibbling, as Tyanna was restraining her arms.

By the time Herman was reaching 7-inch deep strokes, Brea's breathing had become so intense and she was inhaling so deeply that the outline of her rib-cage was visible through her skin. Also, her mouth was wide-open, the skin between her eyebrows wrinkled, the veins in her neck were popping-out and her eyes would shut so tightly that her eyelashes completly disappeared from view.

Trina and I had sucked her nipples so hard and for so long that they were now glowing a bright-reddish hue.

Herman grabbed one hand from me and Trina, put them in his mouth to moisten the finger tips and then placed them at Brea's lower stomach.

Trina didn't hesitate to begin rolling her fingers around Brea's over-sized clit, which made her grunts greatly increase in volume and frequency as her stomach fluttered up-n-down and contracted. After just a few seconds of Trina's finger-tickling, Brea's back arched high enough off the rug for us to roll a basketball under it, and abruptly fell, as I watched her legs shiver and could hear the rattling sound of gritted-teeth. An abundance of Brea's cream had accumulated on Herman's condom from her climax as her lips were constantly quivering.

"Eeee-Eeee-Eeee-Eeee!", Brea cried-out in an ear-pierce squeaky voice at Trina's tortuous hand fanning across her clit faster and faster until her entire body went through a serious of violent jerks as she uttered, "Ohhh Shit! Ohhh SHIT! OOOOH-WHOOOA, SHEEEEEEEEE-ITTTTTTT! I'm cummin, I'm cummin, I'm cummin', ohhhhh"

I had to rescue Brea myself from Trina's still stroking hand, as she'd apparently become addicted to the reaction it caused and wasn't planning on stopping. Brea could do nothing about it herself, as Tyanna was keeping a tight hold on her struggling arms.

When Herman removed himself, Brea's legs clamped shut and shivered from her climax residue.

Herman removed the condom, to replace it with a new one, as he sat on the sofa and beckoned for Trina. Trina faced Herman and straddled her big-ass on him. As she slowly lowered herself on his thang, Herman began chomping her nipples, as Tyanna and a recovering Brea positioned themselves on each side. Tyanna couldn't resist spanking Trina's already shaking and trembling ass cheeks, as Brea copy-cat'd her, doing the same on the other side.

Trina held the backrest of the sofa in a death-grip, as Herman began to pump upward. Tyanna had left her post to retrieve some goodies from the wicker sex-basket. She handed a bottle of oil to me, I guess to keep me involved, and instructed me to pour it all over the back of Trina. All of our hands participated in rubbing the oil on Trina's back, butt and legs, as Brea chose to slide her right hand down the front of Trina's stomach to perform the same task Trina had done to Brea.

As Brea massaged Trina's clit, which caused the natural arch of her back to flatten out a bit, Tyanna grabbed a narrow dildo from the basket and rolled it around Trina's back to moisten it with oil.

Oh no she's not gonna....!, I thought to myself, as Trina looked back over her shoulder to see what was going on.

When Trina didn't say anything, as she turned her head back to facing Herman, Tyanna and Brea gripped one cheek with their hands, as Tyanna teased the dildo up-n-down her seam in paint-brush-strokes-form before gently inserting it in Trina's ass.

"Ohh, shit! Ohhhhh, shit!", Trina cursed at the stimulation and beat-up the backrest of the sofa with her hand, which made me laugh, not only at hearing the obscenity, but witnessing the double penetration.

233

Her thick thighs shook as her head cocked forward like a church-deacon's does while falling asleep during a sermon.

When Brea's hand replaced Tyanna's on the dildo, her competitive-ass acted as though she was in a race with Herman's pumping. She mirrored his depth to the level of Herman's 5-inch strokes and alternated the stroke of the dildo with Herman's stroke. Trina moans instantaneously became thunderous, her body tensed-up as she clutched the backrest so firmly that I could see the tricep-muscles in her arms flexing.

"You gonna cum?", Tyanna asked.

Trina could only turn her tight-jawed head towards Tyanna and nod 'yes' as her response. Just as I'd done for Brea, I saved Trina from Brea's pump-happy ass, placing my hand atop Brea's to pull the dildo out, as a relieved Trina collapsed forward on Herman.

Once the seemingly ever-ready Herman had opened his third condom packet, he attempted to lay me on my back on the rug the way he'd done to Brea, but I wasn't haven't it. Not like that.

My advantage was that I'd gotten to see them first. I chose to ride him like Trina, that way I'd be able to push-up off of him if I needed to in a hurry and avoid having my arms restrained like Brea.

"Mmmmm, mmmmm, mmmm", I moaned like a Campbell's soup commercial as I eased down on him.

Herman's dick made my pussy feel virgin-tight, as it easily touched all the walls.

I covered my butt with my hand before I got too far along into it and spoke.

"Nothing in my butt!", I declared, spinning my head to look Trina, Brea and Tyanna in the face, so that no one could claim they didn't hear me.

Herman's dick was more than enough, all by itself. I wasn't gonna have my concentration broken by worrying about whether someone was planning to shove something in my ass.

Herman squeezed the back of my thighs just below my butt, as I rode him to a depth that ranged up to 7-inches. I flattened my stomach against him to prevent anyone from sliding a tickling hand to my clit. However, it didn't stop Brea and Trina from oiling and spanking my ass while each of them twisted a nipple to ripeness with their other hand and Tyanna tugged on the mane of my hair.

As Herman's pumps ever-gradually raised the cum-factor level in me, I bit my bottom lip so hard that I thought it might leave a scar.

"Ahhh, AhhhH, AhHHH, AHHHHH!", I moaned at the arrival of my climax, as I vaguely heard Trina and Brea laughing about the jolting, jiggling and quaking way I had cum.

When I rolled off of Herman, he got up and removed the condom and rested his back on the bear-skin rug in front of the three of us on the sofa, as Tyanna was preparing to be the finale.

Between me, Trina and Brea, the bottom-half of Herman's dick had been unnecessary, as none of us ventured to a depth of more than 7 of his 14-inches of endowment. That was soon about to change.

The first time of the night that Herman went condom-less was while Tyanna was putting us to shame. She had her back to him, supported herself in a crab-like fashion, with her hands and feet on the rug straddling him, while taking upwards of 11-inches.

We weren't too much ashamed, as after all, this was her husband and she'd obviously had lots of time to get to that level. Even still, it clearly was no simple task for her either, as her eyes wandered with each stroke and her groans were every bit as passionate as ours had been.

Herman supported her back with his hands, as Brea jumped-off the sofa to execute the clit-rubbing technique. The effects of Brea's rubbing on Tyanna had escalated to the point where Tyanna became cross-eyed, with one of her fluttering eyelids closed and the other one half-open, but only the white-part of the eyeball showed, as she screamed that she was indeed cumming.

Further impressing or digusting us, depending on which one of us you asked, Tyanna did the unthinkable and what was thought of as impossible, she took Herman up the butt until she gained his spewing ecstasy, which flowed like it was never gonna cease.

I wanted to get a measuring cup to see just how much cum Herman actually ejected. I ain't lying, it looked like it could've been at least a full cup's-worth.

It goes without saying that tonight was certainly an adventure none of us would soon forget.

Once we dragged ourselves to the other bedroom, the three of our worn-out bodies got some of the best-sleep in our lives.

Chapter Nineteen

The next day, as we were getting dropped-off by Brea at our apartment, after our 'Wild Thangz' night out, Trina and I planned to do nothing but rest and recuperate.

Last night's events were more than just fun to me. It also caused me to reflect on the way the world worked. Sex had been a key to success not only for me, but everything around me that I saw.

It was how Brea was making all of her money, whether it was stripping for ballers like Mr. Whitfield or using it to get financing of a Mercedes.

As for me, it'd gotten me a developmental deal with Joseph Myer, wrestled back to me the lead-singer status with Chocolate Cream, not to mention the job I had at *Reflex*.

And Trina had broken out of her fantasy world and shell of inhibition, because of it.

Though, I did recognize that sex was like fire. If you weren't careful with it, you could get burned too, as how it led to the temporary break-up of our friendship. But over all, the good out-weighed the bad, I thought.

Though we were still tired, Trina and I laughed about last night as we walked down the hallway on our way to our apartment door.

As I turned the key and began opening the door, I was caught off-guard as I was pulled by my arm into the apartment by an unknown man. Trina tried to escape by running, but was quickly caught by another man and brought back into the apartment.

The two muscle-bound white men, restrained us in their arms, with one hand covering our mouths to prevent us from screaming, as a third man casually walked into view from my bedroom.

Our apartment had been trashed. Sofa cushions cut-open, papers thrown everywhere and furniture turned upside down.

Trina and I both continued to struggle to escape our captor's grasp, but they were just too strong. We only stopped, once the slick-back-haired third white man walked up to us and pulled two guns out, from the back of his pants and pointed them at our heads.

"Do you know what these things are at the end of my guns?", the man spoke in a subdued voice, while clicking the ends of the guns together.

Both of our eyes were wide-open from fear, as we shook our heads 'no' because we couldn't answer with our mouths covered.

"These are what they call 'Silencers'. You see, I could shoot you right now and no one would even hear it. Do you understand?", he spoke, as I now noticed his heavy east-coast accent.

We both nodded that we understood.

"I'm gonna have my guys uncover your mouths, but if you so much as scream, I will not hesitate to have them shoot you. However, if you act like good girls and tell us what we want to know, we will not harm you. Do you understand?", he claimed that we had options.

My heart raced as I nodded agreement to him and I felt like I was gonna pee on myself.

The slick-back-haired man, that was obviously the one in charge, nodded to the other guys that it was okay to release us and they did so, cautiously.

As the man in charge put his guns away, his two goons drew their guns, stood off to the side of us and pointed them at our heads as we shivered in fear.

"Relax! I told you, we're not going to hurt you", he said in a soothing tone as a response to our nervous behavior.

"You can have my purse, I don't have much money in there, but take it!", I urged for them to just rob us and leave.

The man's shoulders bounced as he laughed, "Do you think we're thieves? We're not here to rob you"

"Please don't rape us! You can have all of our money!", Trina begged.

"Shhhh. Nobody's gonna rape you", he said walking up to us and gently rubbing a hand down the side of each of our faces. "All I want to know is where's Brea?", he asked.

At that moment, I recognized his voice from the calls with the 718-area code.

"I don't know", I hurried to respond before Trina.

Of the two of us, I was the most street-wise and I figured that he might not keep his promise to leave us alive, if he got what he'd come for. I wanted to make sure that I answered before Trina got us killed.

"See, that's not the answer I'm looking for", he said calmly before violently grabbing our throats in each of his hands tightly. "Let's try this again. Where's Brea? I know that she lives here"

"She don't live here anymore. She moved out. I don't know where she lives, but I can try to find out", I said, trying to give him a reason to leave us alive.

He turned his head to Trina, seeing as I was doing all of the talking up to this point, to see if I was telling the truth. I was nervous as hell, wondering if Trina had a clue as to what she should say.

"She used to live here, but I don't know where she is now", Trina said, causing me to sigh temporary relief.

I was still worried because we could see their faces and they weren't concerned about it, which made me think that they still might kill us. But what we were doing, I felt, was our best option for survival.

He let go of our throats, as he turned his back to us and paced a few steps in thought.

"Marco, you want us to pop them or what?", one of the goons asked nonchalantly.

"No, Bruno. No. I believe them. I don't think they even know what's going on. We'll use them as messengers", Marco said turning back around. "Which one of you is Jazmyn Reneé Wallace with a younger sister, Tyisha, a younger brother, Malcom and parents that live in College Park?"

My eyes widened with surprise of the detailed information that he had about me.

"That must be you", he said at the reading of my facial expression. "So that means you must be Trina Whitfield, the daughter of Michael and Tonya Whitfield", he continued looking at Trina. "I'm sorry to hear about your parents' divorce", he added.

"I on't …. I ….", I struggled to ask the connection he had with us.

He quieted my stumbling by raising his hand to my face, "Yes, I know all about you and where your family lives. Here's the deal Jazmyn and Trina. Your girl Brea has a brother that used to work for us before he went to jail."

"I swear! We don't know nothin' about that!", I interjected.

"Shut up!", screamed Bruno, as he viciously tugged my head backward by my hair.

"Brea's brother, went to jail…", Marco said picking-up where he'd left-off. "Going to jail ain't the problem. Shit, happens. The problem we have is this. The cocaine that was confiscated and the amount of money they found with him don't match-up. So, we know that Brea's brother was skimmin' on us. Somewhere, there's some cocaine or money that belongs to my employer and he wants it, NOW! You girls seem to be bright. And, believe me, we're not animals. We just want what belongs to us. We figure Brea probably has some information about this. I don't care either way. But, I'm gonna get the $80,000 in money or the cocaine. Then, you'll never hear from us again. That's my message I want you to give to Brea. Now I figure, you might not think that you're involved, BUT BOTH OF YOU NOW ARE! And, if I don't get either one, my money or my cocaine, I'm gonna kill both of you, Brea, your families and have Brea's brother killed in jail, cap-eesh?", he informed, using an Italian-ish hand-gesture. "But hey-ayyy, I'm a reasonable man. So here's what I'm gonna do for you. All three of you, have 10-days to get my $80,000 or my cocaine. It's that simple. Oh, you may want to ask Brea about the Vinetti Family before you even think about involving the police. That would be a terrible and most unfortunate mistake on your part. We'll be in touch. 10-days! Let's go guys", he finished his ultimatum and calmly stepped over some of our broken furniture to exit through the front door.

Even after they'd gone, we were so scared that neither of us dared to move to the front door to lock it, or even speak, fearing they may still be outside the door listening. Eventually, after about 10-minutes of silence, I tip-toed over, turned the locks and Trina and I pushed our severely damaged sofa up against the door.

We sat side-by-side on the floor, propped against the other end of the sofa.

I'd wished there was some way that I could just magically blink my eyes and disappear, or that I was able to rewind the clock, so that I not have to experience what just happened.

"We gotta call the police", Trina suggested as she stood-up to go to the phone.

"Shut up!", I yelled as I yanked her back down to the

floor by her arm while I looked over my shoulder and listened to hear if the goons were outside the front door and heard her comments. "Trina! We CAN'T call the police. You heard what they said!"

"Well we gotta do something!", she urged.

She was right, but I didn't know what that 'something' was. So I sat there destroying my manicure by chewing on my finger-nails.

"Alright", I said, having my normal thinking pattern slowly returning. "The first thing we gotta do is talk to Brea. See what she knows about these guys that her brother worked for".

"Oh, shit! We need to warn Brea! They could be headed to her apartment, right now!", Trina unnecessarily worried.

"Calm down Trina! Calm down. If they knew where Brea lived already, they wouldn't have come over here!", I reminded her.

"Oh, yeah. That's right! But we still gotta warn her, so that she doesn't just run into them"

"Yeee-ah, that's true. Shit! How are we gonna get out of here?", I said, thinking out loud.

I was paranoid. I didn't wanna call Brea because I thought the phone may be tapped. Not to mention, now that we were alone and semi-safely locked in the apartment, I didn't wanna venture outside and risk possibly being followed to Brea's apartment.

I knew that none of us should call our parents because I was certain they'd absolutely do the wrong thing ….. call the police.

We decided that we had to leave the apartment and go talk to Brea.

Each of us took turns keeping an eye on the front door while the other hastily packed some clothes in a bag.

Cautiously, we moved the sofa and peeked down the hall. Seeing no one there, we exited our apartment via a back-entrance staircase and walked through a small field behind the apartment building that led to a gas station on the other side. From there, we called a taxi.

We didn't wanna take either one of our cars that were parked in the front of the building, because we thought that they probably knew what we drove and might possibly be sitting in a car waiting so that they could follow us.

Chapter Twenty

We spent $136 on a taxi ride to Brea's apartment that normally would've cost no more that $20.

The added expense was for safety. We made the taxi driver venture in all different directions in Atlanta, as we tried to ascertain whether or not we were being followed.

The taxi driver thought our behavior was strange, but didn't care, as we periodically paid him over the seat as the meter fee continuously got higher. The driver was fine with our erratic and peculiar behavior, as long as he knew that we weren't gonna stiff him on the cab fee. Seeing as we were paying as we drove, he made no issue of it.

After we were sure that we weren't being followed, we gave him the actual address of our destination and soon arrived at Brea's apartment.

We banged on the door several times, but there was no answer.

"Brea! Brea!", I spoke loudly while looking down the hall of her apartment complex to see if anyone was coming.

Trina had just pulled out her cell phone to call Brea, just as she was finally answering the door. We didn't want to call her at all from our cell phones, just in case, but while stranded in the hallway, we figured that we had no choice.

"WHAT IS UP?", Brea whined and squinted, clearly having been awakened from sound-sleeping.

"Gurrl, we gotta talk to you!", I said, as I pushed my way into the apartment, as I leaned back to take one last glance down the hallway. "After you dropped us off, there were these guys in our apartment with guns"

"Whaaaaaaatttt?!", Brea immediately woke-up.

"Your brother owes them some money or somethin' and they said they're gonna kill all of us unless they get $80,000 or their cocaine back", Trina jumped in.

"Oh, shit! Oh, shit! Was it the Vinettis?", Brea asked.

"Yes. How did you know that? Who are they?", I inquired quickly.

"Oh, shit! Oh, shit! What did they say?", Brea seriously questioned.

Brea's intensity served to make me more nervous because she didn't rattle easy and she looked scared.

"Brea! Who are the Vinettis?!", I re-asked my unanswered question.

"Oh shit! Oh, shit!", she repeated as she walked around in a circle, while running her hand through hair. "The Vinettis are this crime family up in New York that my brother had been fuckin' with. He was trying to step-up his game in the drug business to make more money by dealing direct with some of the suppliers. What did they say?"

"They said your brother was skimmin' on them and the money that he got caught with and the drugs don't add up. So they think your brother owes them $80,000", Trina explained.

"Does your brother still have the money somewhere, so that we can pay them?", I asked.

"I don't know! I don't know shit about what he was doing! Oh, shit!", Brea claimed. "See, I told my brother not to fuck with the Vinettis", she whined to herself.

"Brea, I don't give a fuck about that! They said they were gonna kill me and my parents if they don't get their money. They put a fuckin' gun to my head! Can you call them and tell 'em that I ain't involved, or find out where the money is, or something? Shit!", Trina shedded all evidence of her normally meek demeanor.

"Yeah", I added.

"I don't know them. I just know of them", she responded disappointingly.

"Well, can you call your brother or something? They said that they're gonna kill us in 10-days if they don't get their money or the cocaine back. Shit! Do something! This shit don't involve me or Trina, that's your brother, but now they got our parents address and shit!", I raised my voice at Brea.

"My brother's in jail! I can't just call him! He has to

call me......", Brea attempted to explain.

"Well, have someone in your family go see him to get this shit straightened-out!", I impatiently interrupted. "In the meantime, we're gonna stay right here, 'cause they don't know where you live yet. We are definitely not going back to our apartment until this shit gets cleared up. Hell, I'on't know if we goin' ever go back!"

Brea made a call to her parents' in Brooklyn to try to find out if they'd been contacted, which she doubted or she would've already been called by them. At the same time, we told her not to inform them of the situation if they weren't aware, because they might call the police and cause me, Trina and our families to die.

Brea's parents were obviously unaware because they spoke only about the fact that she'd not called home in a while.

The fact that they'd not been contacted made me wonder, why would the Vinettis come all the way to Atlanta, when Brea's parents lived right there in Brooklyn? Maybe the Vinetti Family was scared of the police and that was the right thing to do?

I analyzed the shit out of this situation.

It seemed like Brea was telling the truth about not knowing anything, but I knew Brea, and it was possible that she could be lying.

However, making her story more believable was when I reflected on how she'd moved to Atlanta in the first place. She'd admitted that she'd used the few thousands of dollars from her brother's drug money to move, but it was far from $80,000. Plus, knowing Brea, there was no way she'da had 80-grand and not have already bought a car, so I believed her.

At a stand-still on decision making, Trina and I settled in to Brea's apartment as we all were quietly in thought over the next half-hour, trying to figure a way out of this mess.

I went through several options in my head, but none were all that sound of an idea.

Finally, it was decided that Brea would fly back to New York to try to find out more information from her brother's crew, or see if she'd be able to get visitation at the prison so she could try to find out where the money or the cocaine was, though it was doubtful that she'd be able to get visitation on such short notice.

Brea booked a Priceline.com ticket and prepared to fly-out tomorrow on Monday and would be returning early Wednesday morning. In the evening of that same day, I was supposed to be flying to Los Angeles for the movie cameo shoot for the band.

Trina and I shared Brea's Mercedes, not willing to risk more contact with the Vinettis by attempting to get our cars from our apartment.

The only places we went were to *Reflex* to work and to the studio, as Trina didn't wanna ever be alone until the situation had been settled.

Over the next three days, it was like sitting on pins and needles waiting to hear from Brea when she returned. All kinds of thoughts were constantly going through my head.

I wondered, was Brea gonna come back or leave us

hanging while she hid in Brooklyn? I didn't think she'd do that, but the thought did cross my mind more than once.

Before she'd left, I'd mentioned to her about Brandon's background and that maybe he could help us take care of the problem with the thugs that he employed. But Brea made it very clear that the Vinettis were way out of his league and Brandon's involvement would surely get us killed.

Then I thought about Trina's parents. They had money, although it was tied-up because of their divorce proceedings. But they'd surely agree to un-freeze it if they knew it would save their daughter's life, not to mention their own, I thought. However, the risk was too great to involve them, as we again thought about how they'd involve the police first, before just giving 80-grand of their money to some thugs as debt repayment for Brea's brother.

When we didn't hear from Brea on Monday or Tuesday, I really began to worry if she'd actually be at the airport on Wednesday morning when we went to pick her up.

Though to be honest, we had all agreed that she shouldn't call us, instead deliver the news in person. But I couldn't help but think that if she had good news, how would she be able to resist calling?

On Wednesday morning, we eagerly watched the escalators, as we waited for Brea to emerge from the sea of arriving airline passengers.

Secretly, I know Trina and I both hoped that Brea would come into view with a huge smile on her face that would signal that everything was gonna be okay. Neither one of us said anything to each other, I guess we didn't wanna jinx it. After a lot of passengers passed us, my secret thought concerning Brea possibly not returning began to surface.

Then, we did see her, but not the smile. Not a frown either. So I couldn't tell what the deal was.

"Hey, Brea??", I greeted her, quickly.

"Hey Jaz. Hey Trina.", she said not giving any news that she must've known that we were dying to hear.

"What's up, Brea? Did you get the money or the cocaine?", Trina bluntly asked.

"SHHHH! Not here!", Brea urged.

"Bullshit, Brea. What's up?!!", I stopped her from walking to the baggage-claim area by grabbing her by the elbow and demanded for her to delay no longer. "What'dya find out?!"

"It's gonna be okay.", she claimed.

"How?? Did you get the money or what?", I sternly asked.

"Yes and no. I got it worked out. Trust me, I can't tell you while we're in the airport!", Brea commanded in a hard whisper.

"As soon as we get to the car, I wanna know what the hell is going on!", I ruggedly conceded, as Trina and I impatiently helped collect her bags and we all caught the shuttle van to the parking lot.

We couldn't talk in the shuttle van because there were other people.

"What the fuck is up?", Trina questioned, the moment we sat in Brea's Mercedes.

"I talked to a couple of my brothers friends and they said that they didn't know anything!", Brea began.

"And you believed them?! Oh, fuck, Brea!", Trina whined disappointment that we'd lost three days on the Vinetti's 10-day deadline.

"You said it was gonna be alright. How?", I asked, hanging-on for any glimmer of hope.

"I thought of a plan for how we're going to get the money", Brea said confidently.

I was scared and not nearly as confident about what Brea had in mind. But I was desperate, so I asked, "What's the plan?"

Chapter Twenty-One

The four of us all took deep breaths, as we sat in my car that was parked in the front lot of the building. I couldn't believe it had come to this.

It was the middle of Saturday night. Technically, it was 3 A.M. on Sunday morning. I'd just gotten off a plane less than 10-hours ago, returning from the California movie shoot.

We'd just completed Phase-1 of Brea's plan and it was too late to back-out now. Especially, when we knew that there was just 3-days left of the Vinetti's deadline.

"Let's just go!", Trina said, not being able to take the wait any longer and recognizing that we only had another 90-minutes in our window of opportunity.

"Wait", I said, wanting to make sure everything went

smoothly. "Trina, do you have the bags?"

"Yes", she sighed, while holding them up.

"Brea are you sure you remember the ......", I attempted to ask.

"Yes! I got it!", Brea cut me off. "Just relax, Jaz!"

Her abrasive tone of words made me angry. I wouldn't even be here tonight if it weren't for her. But I swallowed my fury, knowing it was best to focus, rather than argue.

We opened all four doors at the same time and got out of my car. Each of us tried to close our door quietly, but the combined sound of them closing together, at the same time, echoed louder than expected in the still night air.

Even with something as minor as a little extra unexpected noise, I began feeling like it was a sign that our plan was already doomed. All four of us were rookies.

"Jaz, did you just lock the car doors?", Brea asked.

"Oh, shit! Habit", I tried to explain apologetically, as the three of them had to wait for me to walk back to my car and unlock all four doors.

"Hurry up, Jaz!", Trina whispered, mindful of the time on her watch. "We only have 86-minutes left"

In my haste, I damn near broke my neck, as I slipped when I accidentally stepped into a spot of oil that was on the ground.

"Shit, Jaz! Be careful!", Brea berated my mis-step. "C'mon!"

We all put on our latex gloves provided by Trina and pulled down our masks, as Brea unlocked the front door with the key. The alarm blared so loudly, that I began sweating. It was just a matter of seconds before Brea had quieted the alarm by punching in the code.

Now inside of *Reflex*, we waited for Brea to punch the code in to the vault, as Jamal stood guard at the front door until it was time to open the heavy vault door.

I'd strong-arm-recruited Jamal into our plan, threatening that he'd be in jail on statutory-rape charges for having sex with Tyisha if he didn't help us.

After Jamal used his muscles to open the vault door, Trina and I hurriedly began stuffing cash into our bags, as Brea found the surveillance tape recorder and Jamal resumed his look-out post.

Once Brea'd retrieved the tape, she handed it to Jamal, which freed her hands to help stuff the bags.

The filled-bags were heavier than we'd thought, which made it necessary that Jamal would have to carry all four bags to the car, which wasn't the original plan.

"Jaz, leave the bags right here. You just go get the car and pull it right up to the door", Jamal instructed.

As I got into the car, a police car was doing a routine drive-through of the parking lot.

"Oh, shit! Oh, shit! Oh, shit!", I nervously chanted to myself while leaning down in the front seat out of view.

Just before leaning down, I was glad to see that Jamal, Trina and Brea had seen the police car as it pulled into the lot, as they scurried to hide behind the wall inside of *Reflex*.

The police car rolled agonizingly slowly through the lot as it shined its spot light into the windows of each business window along the strip-mall.

My heart was pounding so loudly, I thought the noise of it beating would give me away.

While the police officer's attention was focused on the store-windows, a few doors down from Reflex, I peeked my head up to notice that one bag of money was suspiciously sitting in the front of the store, directly in view.

The police car slowed for a moment as his light shined on the bag. The officer exited the car and started walking to the window.

Just as the officer reached to check the door, that I knew was unlocked, the officer's hand went instead to the walkie-talkie hooked to his shoulder and spoke into it.

I couldn't watch anymore, as I re-ducked my head and used my ears as my eyes.

I heard the sound of a door closing, which made me look-up again. Thankfully, the officer was in his car and speeding out of the parking lot. Apparently he'd just gotten a more urgent call.

Even after I was pretty sure that the cop was gone, I remained slumped in the car, doing a body-check to see if I was having a heart-attack or not. I was having trouble getting a sufficient amount of air in my lungs, my armpits were dripping with sweat and my chest was pounding. I closed my eyes to try to calm myself.

Clack! Clack! Clack!, I heard the sound of a flashlight banging against my window.

Any progress I'd made towards subduing myself was now lost, as I jerked from the noise.

Whew!, I exhaled. It was Jamal.

"Jazmyn! Bring the fuckin' car around!", he said irate.

"Okay!", I screamed back, but wasn't at all as cool about the situation as him.

Once I pulled the car in front of the building, Jamal loaded the heavy cash-filled bags in the trunk, while Trina got in the back seat.

Brea locked the front door of Reflex and also got in the car, as Jamal left the front passenger door open. He took a crowbar out of the trunk, cocked his arm back and smashed the front door glass to make it look like a random robbery, before hopping in the car.

"Let's go!", he said, as I pulled off before he'd even closed his car door completely.

I didn't turn the headlights on for at least a block.

We'd driven about ten minutes when Jamal nervously twisted in the front seat, reaching under it and said, "Oh, FFFFF-FUCK!"

"What?! What?!", I spoke with concern.

"Pull over, NOW!", Jamal demanded and I did as told. "Pop the trunk!"

Jamal got out and looked in the trunk for a minute before returning disappointed as he plopped into the front seat.

"What's wrong?", Trina leaned forward to Jamal.

"After that cop came around, I forgot the tape!", Jamal admitted his blunder.

"It don't matter. We had masks on", Brea began arguing for us not to go back.

"Yeah, but how's that gonna work with the plan?", Jamal said with concern for him.

"We can't go back! That's just asking to get caught. We got the money, let's just keep going!", I urged.

"No!", Trina screamed her opinion, not wanting to leave evidence, even if our faces weren't shown on the tape. "We GOTTA get the tape!"

Me and Brea wanted to keep going, while Jamal and Trina were adamant about returning to the scene of our crime.

After 3-minutes of loud conversation, we compromised that we'd drive by *Reflex* to check it out.

Just as we rolled past the strip-mall, me and Brea were proven right, as three police cars were already investigating the scene with their lights flashing on the squad cars.

All of our heads faced forward, as I drove right by without drawing attention because the strip-mall was set-back a nice distance from the street.

We were very silent on the way to drop Jamal off at his car, so that he could transfer the bags of money into it that we'd retrieve from him later.

Trina was still nervous because we were late in getting back to Hung and Sumy's house, which was Phase-3 of our plan.

Chapter Twenty-Two

Brea used the key to cautiously open the door of Hung and Sumy's house. We were relieved to see that they were lying, just as we'd left them, in the bedroom.

Trina, Brea and I stripped naked and found a place to sleep in the bedroom. Well, pretended that we were asleep until the morning.

For us not to be professional criminals, we'd come up with what was to be a rather ingenious 3-Phase plan.

After Brea had no success in New York, she'd thought about where we could get money in the amount of $80,000. Obviously, a bank robbery she ruled-out. And trying to gold-dig it from even the plethora of ballers that she was fucking was far too slow and risky.

She'd come to the conclusion that there were only two places that had that kind of cash on hand. *Reflex* and *Slick-N-Thick*.

After informing me and Trina of her plan for a robbery, we were frightened of even the idea. Even more so, by the fact that a robbery was Brea's best idea to keep us from getting killed.

As long as we'd known each other, Brea always had the plan. Whether it was getting money from the director of a shoot in Miami, convincing a man to provide 'creative' financing for her Mercedes, using her connections to be the star in music videos, or hookin' us up with jobs at *Reflex*, Brea always had the plan.

Between *Reflex* and *Slick-N-Thick*, we thought the better of the two was *Reflex*.

We ruled-out stealing from *Slick-N-Thick* for two reasons.

First, *Slick-N-Thick* didn't close until 4 A.M. and wasn't totally empty until an hour after that. The 1st-shift bartenders would be in as early as 9 or 10 preparing to open the club at Noon. Therefore, the window for theft would be a very small one. Not to mention that there were two time-locked steel doors that we'd have to get through before we got to the money.

The second reason was that there was definitely more risk of retribution associated with stealing from Herman and Tyanna. If we got caught, the police would be the last thing we'd have to worry about.

Knowing the free and freaky nature of Hung and Sumy, we'd decide that it would be them that we'd rob.

Brea's nosey ass had already previously viewed surveillance tapes, even before we knew of the problems we had with the Vinettis. I couldn't believe that she'd done that, as it indicated that she'd already pre-meditated a theft of her own. However, having been in the situation we were in, it was a good thing.

From the tapes, she'd been able to see the codes that Hung and Sumy punched for the security system and the vault as well.

Our 'Wild Thangz' party experience inspired the way that we'd be able to obtain keys to the front door.

Hung's and Sumy's free and freaky nature made it almost a sure bet that they'd be down with a private 'Wild Thangz' party suggestion that included me, Trina and Brea.

Just as we predicted, they were gung-ho about the spur-of-the-moment idea, suggested to them by Brea, on the Thursday after Brea got back from New York.

The party was all set for Saturday night at Hung's and Sumy's home.

Being a Pre-Med major, Trina was able to steal some Chloralhydrate from the Med-Facility at Spellman. Chloralhydrate is a liquid chemical used to harmlessly sedate a person for several hours, which would be just enough time for us to steal the keys from Hung, drive to *Reflex*, empty the vault and return to their home without them ever knowing that we'd left.

We figured that when the police discovered the break-in, suspicion would obviously be that of an inside-job, first.

Our plan would make for the owners, Hung and Sumy, to actually provide the alibi for us. As far as they'd be aware, we were at their home all night, during the time of the robbery.

Jamal was added for safety, just in case we ran into problems.

The plan was a simple one. During our *'Wild Thangz'* escapade with Hung and Sumy, Trina poured some of the Chloralhydrate into their drinks.

While they were unconscious, we stole the keys, broke into *Reflex*, met Jamal at a nearby hotel parking lot, he jumped in my car as it was the least fancy of all, took the cash from the vault, re-locked the front door, broke the glass to make it look like it was random, then returned to Hung's and Sumy's house, so that it'd not appear that we'd never left.

For the most part, our plan went off without too many problems. However, leaving the tape which clearly outlined the thieves by gender was the one glitch. But, there was nothing that we could do about that now.

On Sunday morning, Hung and Sumy were awakened by a phone call from the police informing them that their business and been burglarized.

"I'm sorry! We gotta go!", Hung said after informing us of the subject of the phone call he'd just ended.

"I can't believe that!", Brea acted surprised. "Do you want us to go with you?"

"Awwh, shit!", Hung exhaled frustration, pre-occupied thinking about the worst. "Um, no. Ahhh, we just gotta go. I'm sorry to kick you guys out, but we gotta go!"

"Oh, no problem! We understand!", I added.

Trina's face wasn't as convincing as me and Brea's so I was glad that Hung and Sumy were in a dazed state, otherwise they would've picked-up on it.

We collected our things and left.

"Call us later to let us know what happened", Brea portrayed concern.

"I will", Hung said, as he and Sumy were hastily trying to do minimum grooming before they left as well.

"Whew! $112,000!", Jamal excitedly spoke the total of our take at the hotel room he'd rented.

Jamal knew about the reason for the robbery.

"I'm just glad that it's enough to pay the Vinettis!", Trina said with relief.

"Yeah, but that leaves an extra 32-grand. Split four-ways, that's 8-grand a piece!", Jamal suggested, as Brea was busy holding one of the bundles of cash.

"I don't want any of it!", Trina claimed. "I just want to pay the Vinettis and be done!"

"Fine with me!", Brea hurried to say. "That's about 10-grand each, three-ways"

"Hold up!", I said before they got to far in their plans. "I say that we give it ALL to the Vinettis. Let's make sure that they won't kill us! We'll call it interest!"

"Are you out of your fuckin' mind?", Jamal yelled. "I'on't risk going to jail to not get anything out of it".

"No! You did it to not go to jail for Statutory Rape! There was no deal about the money!", I screamed back.

"That's bullshit! I'ma get some of this money!", Jamal charged standing over me to intimidate.

"Chill, Jamal!", Brea said, stepping between me an Jamal, pushing him back with his forearm.

As he walked back to the table of loot, Brea spoke softly to me.

"Jaz. If we pay them their $80,000 the Vinettis won't do anything. I know their reputation. Trust me, it's gonna be okay!", Brea try to convince.

Her comments fell on deaf-ears, as I recognized that she couldn't really guarantee me shit! She didn't know them like that. I wasn't willing to bet my life on what she thought might be true.

Trina was behind me 100%, after hearing my idea about an extra incentive for the Vinettis to leave us alive.

We argued ferociously, before Trina and I finally came to the conclusion that we could use our share of the money to put with the $80,000, making it now a total of $96,000 that we'd hand-over on Tuesday to the Vinettis when they returned to collect.

We were pissed that Brea and Jamal didn't comply, but we also thought that our goal would be achieved with the extra 16-grand.

Chapter Twenty-Three

On Tuesday-morning, Trina, Brea and I were in me and Trina's apartment with the $96,000 in cash we were waiting to give to the Vinettis when they returned. We cleaned the apartment that'd been previously left in shambles, as a way to work off nervous energy.

All three of us were dressed in the sexiest outfits, we had. Three sets of bossoms over-flowing out of tops and legs shined with lotion and showing-off in short mini-skirts. We'd hope that the added sex-appeal would make it difficult for them to kill us. Well, that's what we hoped.

The loud knock on our door caused us all to be extremely nervous, even Brea.

We'd spent our time trying to come-up with all the

reasons why today would not be the last day of our existence. But the truth was none of us knew that for sure.

I went to the door and opened it, as Bruno and the other goon quickly pushed me to the side and spun their heads around to survey our apartment, before Marco entered.

"Nice of you to join us, Brea", Marco spoke at the mere sight of the new female in the room, as though he already knew her.

It was clear that Brea hadn't lied to us about not knowing him, as her face was surprised that he'd identified her by face, not realizing that it was simply from deduction. Marco knew who we were, so that meant the new female had to be Brea.

"Hi-iigh", Brea's voice cracked in response.

"Do you guys have what we came for?", Marco asked while his goons were busy checking the other rooms to make sure that we were alone.

"Yes!", Trina said anxious to execute the transaction and for them to leave.

Brea and Trina kept an eye-out on the goons as I retrieved a duffle bag containing the 96-G's from under the kitchen sink.

"Here it is!", I cautiously handed to him from as far of a distance that I could extend my arm.

"I hope you're not offended by my counting it?", Marco said rather calmly, like this was a legitimate business deal.

The delay of their exit by taking the time to count the money in our apartment scared us. We weren't sure if they were gonna kill us after counting it or not. But the calm tone of Marco's voice made me hold-out hope that it wasn't the case. Plus I figured, when he first unzipped the bag and saw the cash, he could've just done it right then, but he didn't.

First, Marco fanned through each stack to make sure that the whole stack was actual money and not the inside filled with blank paper. Next, he had Bruno and the other goon meticulously start counting, while his attention was steadfastly on our whereabouts.

"Did you guys get all dressed up for me?", he laughed at our apparently veil and rookie-ish attempt.

"Umm-hmm", Brea seductively hummed, as my jaws tightened from not knowing what-in-the-hell she was trying to do.

"Oh, there's an extra 16-grand in the bag!", Brea more comfortably explained, as though she'd contributed to the extra money.

During her comments, she'd even dared to take a couple of steps in his direction like she was becoming relaxed with the situation.

The goons looked up for a minute, distracted by Brea's swaying toward Marco.

"Hey! Pay attention to what you're fuckin' doing! Count the shit!", Marco chastised them both.

Marco's eye resumed targeting Brea's chest, as Brea eye-balled him back.

Trina and I stood there like little sisters that'd been dragged out on our big sisters date. My legs were shaking, as I couldn't believe what I was witnessing from Brea, but didn't have the courage to stop her. Besides feared Marco's reaction if I did, as he didn't seem to mind the game.

Though, it was clear Brea wasn't capable of making him forget what he came to do, whatever that was.

As Brea stood in front of Marco talking, arching her back, with her butt and chest sticking out and her hand on her hip, Marco smiled as though he was really laughing at her. He nonchalantly looked at the table to see the progress the goons were making on the count before reaching up to Brea's top, not even concerned about permission, and pulled it down until both of her titties popped out.

Brea's hand briefly left her hip, as though it intended to do something about what he'd done, as I think she didn't expect that he'd be that bold. But her hand never made it all the way up to his hand and she put it back on her hip trying to recover like she'd not be surprised at all by his aggressive move.

What in the fuck is Brea doing?!! She's gonna get us killed or raped or something bad!, I thought loudly in my head.

Reading Trina's easily readable face, I knew the same thing was running through her head as well.

I was pissed because Brea was always executing plans that she didn't give notice to us before-hand.

Marco pinched Brea's nipples so hard with one hand until her folded lips gave way to attempted-to-be-held-in grunts.

"Awwhhhh! Awwhhh!", she grunted, as Marco squeezed and twisted in a manner that couldn't have been comfortable.

It was obvious that Marco was testing his boys, as they dared not look-up like they wanted to. At the same time, he was teaching Brea a lesson about trying to play her weak-game of seduction on him.

"Ohhhhh! Please! Please! Please!", Brea begged to the determined Marco, that now had her nipples fire-engine red in color.

The pressure from his two-fingered grip was so tight, Brea's standing body jerked forward, while her hands were up like she wanted to grab his, but didn't dare judging by his merciless facial expression.

"You wanna play with me? Do you think I can be played with?", Marco spoke with gritted teeth for Brea's lack of respect for his intelligence, as he forcefully twisted Brea's peaks some more until her legs began dancing from the pain.

"No! No! Please! Please!", Brea again humbly begged Marco to release her, as I could now see that his pliers-like grip had forced a white milky secretion out of her nipple's ends.

"$96,000! It's all here!", Bruno was happy to inform, now free to turn around without verbal abuse from Marco.

Marco didn't even look his way, as he stared at Brea's humbled flushed face for a moment.

"Don't you ever think that you can play with someone like me! You got that?!", he said, as he finally released her, by pushing her back towards us.

Brea's eyes were filled tears and about to overflow as she gingerly tried to stuff her titties back into her top without hurting the already sore nipples.

I didn't like the mood that she'd just created, especially now that they were done counting.

The three of them went to the door and turned around to face us.

"Should I pop 'em now or what?", Bruno asked to Marco while pulling out his gun.

Marco's face was still showing signs of anger at Brea as he scowled at her, before turning his head to look at me and Trina.

"You know what? Forghetta 'bout it", he said, lowering Bruno's raised gun-pointing hand. "These fuckin' bitches got the point!"

The moment they closed the door behind them, my body convulsed in epileptic seizure fashion.

I couldn't fathom how close that I'd just come to death. Every part of my body trembled and shook.

All three of us broke-down crying in tears. And none of us was in any shape to help comfort one another.

Chapter Twenty-Four

The loud clacking sound caused my shoulders to jerk out of pure nervousness, as I lifted my head and glanced over to three empty seats next to me -- seats that were supposed to have been filled.

I was dressed in the finest conservative business attire that I had in my closet and my hair was flawless.

Ordinarily, I'd be feeling good about the way I looked today and about having so many eyes on me. But, it was definitely not an ordinary day. Today's reason for my special costuming had robbed it of its meaning. It was just plain necessary.

I was in court, facing 2-years on Breaking and Entering charges being defend for free by Mrs. Whitfield, Trina's mom. The three empty seats should've been filled by my co-conspirators, Brea, Trina and Jamal, but they hadn't been caught.

Mrs. Whitfield assured me that the prosecution really had no case, but I was still nervous just the same.

Six days after the robbery, I'd been identified as having been in the vault through an oily shoe print that was found inside it. Unknowingly, I'd tracked some of the oil I'd stepped in, the night of the robbery. Supposedly, I'd never been in the vault before, so the presence of my shoe print was difficult to explain.

Besides the embarrassment of my parents having to support me in court, it was another visitor that concerned me the most. Bruno, one of the Vinetti Family goons, was seated in the very last row of the court room looking very interested in the proceedings. I'm sure the Vinetti Family was very interested in whether or not I was going to crack under the pressure of the charges.

After I was caught and arrested, Trina confessed to her mom about the situation, which made her be extremely concerned about my welfare, as her daughter's was directly linked to whatever I said or didn't say. Therefore, she was the one that bailed me out and was representing me, free of charge.

Though I'd been pre-warned that today wouldn't be a long day, it didn't diminish the fact that I hadn't heard someone call me by my full name, Jazmyn Reneé Wallace, since high school home-room roll-call.

The next words out of my mouth would be the most important sentence that I'd ever utter.

The judge woke me out of my daze by asking me yet again, "Ms. Wallace, how do you plead?"

My shaking voice struggled and cracked as I vocalized a simple two-word response.

"Not Guilty!"

Fun Facts!
ABOUT THIS BOOK

- 64,234 Words

MUSIC CD'S PLAYED DURING WRITING OF THIS NOVEL:

Soul Sophisticated
Varied Artist

World Wide Underground
Erykah Badu

College Dropout
Kanye West

The Black Album
Jay-Z

THE COVER

DESIGN & LAYOUT: CANDACE K.
(WWW.CCWEBDEV.COM)

PHOTOS: PATRICK PRIOLEAU (FRONT COVER)

CHARLES A. BROWN (BACK COVER)
(WWW.CABIMAGES.COM)
PUBLISHER PROMO CODE: WT3029

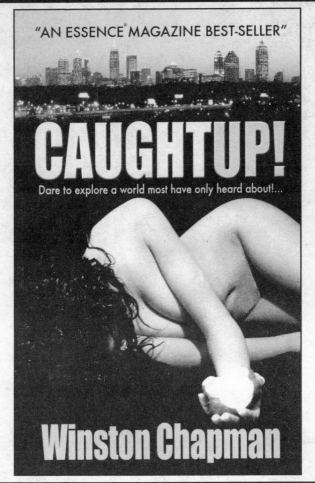